WHY I'M AFRAID OF BEES

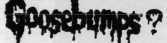

Goosebumps®

WHY I'M AFRAID OF BEES

R.L. STINE

SCHOLASTIC INC.
New York Toronto London Auckland Sydney
Mexico City New Delhi Hong Kong Buenos Aires

ISBN 0-439-69354-3

The *Goosebumps* book series created by Parachute Press, Inc.
Published by Scholastic Inc.
SCHOLASTIC, GOOSEBUMPS,
and associated logos are trademarks and/or registered
trademarks of Scholastic Inc.

24 23 22 21 20 19 18 17 16 15 14 13   13 14 15 /0

Printed in the U.S.A.   40

WHY I'M AFRAID OF BEES

1

If you're afraid of bees, I have to warn you —
there are a *lot* of bees in this story. In fact, there
are hundreds.

Up until last month, I was afraid of bees. And
when you read this story, you'll see why.

It all started in July when I heard a frightening
buzz, the buzz of a bee.

I sat up straight and searched all around. But
I couldn't see any bees anywhere. The scary buzzing sound just wouldn't stop. In fact, it seemed
to be getting louder.

"It's probably Andretti again," I told myself.
"Ruining my day, as usual."

I'd been reading a stack of comic books under
the big maple tree in my back yard. Other kids
might have better things to do on a hot, sticky
summer afternoon — like maybe going to the pool
with their friends.

But not me. My name is Gary Lutz, and I have

to be honest. I don't have many real close friends. Even my nine-year-old sister, Krissy, doesn't like me very much. My life is the pits.

"Why is that?" I constantly ask myself. "What exactly is wrong with me? Why do all the kids call me names like Lutz the Klutz? Why does everybody always make fun of me?"

Sometimes I think it might be because of the way I look. That morning, I'd spent a long time studying myself in the mirror. I'd stared at myself for at least half an hour.

I saw a long, skinny face, a medium-sized nose, and straight blond hair. Not exactly handsome, but not terrible.

Bzzzzzz.

I can't stand that sound! And it was coming even closer.

I flopped over on my stomach. Then I peered around the side of the maple tree. I wanted to get a better view of my neighbor's yard.

Oh, no, I thought. I was right. The buzzing sound was coming from Mr. Andretti's bees. My neighbor was at it again. He was always hanging out in the back by his garage, messing with those bees of his.

How could he handle them every day without worrying about getting stung? I asked myself. Didn't they give him the creeps?

I climbed to my knees and edged a few inches

2

forward. Even though I wanted to get a better look at Mr. Andretti, I didn't want him to see me.

The last time he caught me watching him, he made a big deal out of it. He acted as if there were some kind of law against sitting outside in your own back yard!

"What's this?" he bellowed at the top of his lungs. "Did someone start a neighborhood watch committee without informing me? Or is the FBI recruiting ten-year-old spies these days?"

This last remark really steamed me, because Mr. Andretti knows perfectly well that I'm *twelve* years old. After all, my family has lived next door to him for my entire life. Which is bad luck for me. Mainly since I'm afraid of bees.

I might as well confess it right away. I'm scared of a few other things, too, such as: dogs, big mean kids, the dark, loud noises, and swimming in the ocean. I'm even scared of Claus. That's Krissy's dumb cat.

But, most of all, I'm scared of bees. Unfortunately, with a beekeeper for a neighbor, there are *always* bees around. Hairy, crawly, buzzing, stinging bees.

"*Meow!*"

I jumped up as Claus the cat came creeping up behind me. "Why do you have to stalk me like that?" I cried.

As I spoke, Claus moved forward and wrapped

3

himself around my leg. Then he dug his long, needle-sharp claws into my skin.

"Ouch!" I screamed. "Get away from me!" I cannot understand how Krissy can love that creature so much. She says he only jumps on me because he "likes" me. Well, all I can say is that I *don't* like him! And I wish he would keep away from me!

When I finally managed to chase Claus away, I went back to studying my neighbor. Yes, I'm scared of bees. And I'm fascinated by them, too.

I can't seem to stop watching Mr. Andretti all the time. At least he keeps his hives in a screened-in area behind his garage. That makes me feel pretty safe. And he acts as if he knows what he's doing. In fact, he acts as if he's the world's greatest living expert on bees!

Today, Mr. Andretti was wearing his usual bee outfit. It's a white suit, and a hat with a wire-screen veil hanging down to protect his face. His clothes are tied with string at the wrists and ankles. He looks just like some kind of alien creature out of a horror movie.

As my neighbor carefully opened and closed the drawerlike sections of his hanging hives, I noticed he wasn't wearing any gloves.

Once, when I was with my dad, Mr. Andretti had explained this to us. "It's like this, Lutz," he said. Lutz is my father, Ken Lutz. Naturally, during this entire conversation, Mr. Andretti had acted as if I wasn't even there.

"Your average beekeepers usually wear gloves," he explained. "A lot of the brave ones use gloves with no fingers and thumbs so they can work with the bees more easily."

Mr. Andretti thumped himself on the chest and went on. "But your truly outstanding beekeeper — such as myself — likes to work with his bare hands. My bees trust me. You know, Lutz, bees are really a lot smarter than most people realize."

Oh, sure, I said to myself at the time. If they're really so smart, why do they keep coming back to your hive and letting you steal all their honey from them?

Bzzzzzz.

The humming from Mr. Andretti's hives suddenly grew louder and more threatening. I stood up and walked over to the fence between our two back yards. I gazed into the screened-in area to see what was going on.

Then I gasped out loud.

Mr. Andretti's white suit didn't appear white anymore. It had become *black*!

Why? Because he was totally *covered* with bees!

As I stared, more and more of the insects oozed out of their hives. They crawled all over Mr. Andretti's arms and chest, and even on his head.

I was so grossed out, I thought I might puke!

5

Mr. Andretti's hat and veil shimmered and bulged as if they were *alive*!

Wasn't he scared of all those stingers?

As I leaned over the fence, Andretti suddenly yelled at me: *"Gary — look out!"*

I froze. "Huh?"

"The bees!" Mr. Andretti screamed. "They're out of control! Run!"

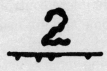

I never ran so fast in my life! I charged across the yard and stumbled up the back steps of my house.

I flung open the screen door and almost fell into the house. Then I stopped and leaned against the kitchen table, gasping for air.

When I finally caught my breath, I listened hard. I could still hear the angry buzzing of the bees from the next yard. Then I heard something else.

"Haw haw haw!"

Somebody was laughing out there. And it sounded suspiciously like Mr. Andretti.

Slowly, I turned around and peered out through the screen door. My neighbor was standing at the bottom of the back steps. He'd taken off his bee veil, and I could see that he had a huge grin on his face.

"Haw haw! You should have seen the expression on your face, Gary. You never would believe how funny you looked! And the way you *ran!*"

I stared at him. "You mean your bees weren't escaping?"

Mr. Andretti slapped his knee. "Of course they weren't! I have complete control of those bees at all times. They come and go, bringing nectar and pollen back from the flowers."

He paused to wipe some sweat off his forehead. "Of course, sometimes I have to go out and re-capture a few lost bees with my net. But most of them know my hives are really the best home they can possibly have!"

"So this was all a joke, Mr. Andretti?" I tried to sound angry. But that's hard to do when your voice is shaking even harder than your knees! "It was supposed to be funny?"

"I guess that'll teach you to get a life and stop staring at me all day!" he replied. Then he turned and walked away.

I was so angry! What a mean trick!

It was bad enough having kids my age pick on me all the time. But now the grown-ups were starting in!

I pounded my fist on the kitchen table just as my mother walked into the room. "Hi, Gary," she said, frowning. "Try not to destroy the furniture, okay? I was just about to make myself a sandwich. Would you like one?"

8

"I guess so," I muttered, sitting down at the table.

"Would you like the usual?"

I nodded. "The usual" was peanut butter and jelly, which I never get tired of. For a snack, I usually like taco chips, the spicier the better. As I waited for my sandwich, I ripped open a new bag of chips and started chewing away.

"Uh-oh." Mom was rummaging through the refrigerator. "I'm afraid we're out of jelly. Guess we'll have to use something else."

She pulled out a small glass jar. "How about this with your peanut butter?"

"What is it?" I asked.

"Honey."

"Honey!" I shrieked. *"No way!"*

Later, I was feeling lonely. I wandered over to the school playground. As I walked by the swing set, I saw a bunch of kids I knew from school.

They were standing around on the softball diamond, choosing up sides for a game. I joined them. Maybe, just maybe, they'd let me play.

"Gail and I are captains," a boy named Louie was saying.

I walked over and stood at the edge of the group. I was just in time.

One by one, Louie and Gail picked players for their teams. Every kid was chosen. Every kid except one, that is. I was left standing by myself next to home plate.

As I slumped my shoulders and stared down at the ground, the captains starting fighting over me. "You take him, Gail," Louie said.

"No. *You* take him."

"No fair. I always get stuck with Lutz!"

As the two captains argued over who was going to be stuck with me, I could feel my face getting redder and redder. I wanted to leave. But then they all would have said I was a quitter.

Finally, Gail sighed and rolled her eyes. "Oh, all right," she said. "We'll take him. But remember the special Lutz rule. He gets *four* strikes before he's out!"

I swallowed hard and followed my teammates out onto the diamond. At that point, luck was with me. Gail sent me to the outfield.

"Go way out in right, Lutz," Gail ordered. "By the back fence. Nobody ever hits it out there."

Some kids might be angry about being stuck so far away from the action. But I was grateful. If no balls were hit to me, I wouldn't have a chance to drop them the way I always did.

As I watched the game, my stomach slowly tied itself into a tight knot. I was last in the batting order. But when my turn at the plate finally came around, the bases were loaded.

I picked up the bat and wandered out toward

the plate. A groan rose up from my teammates. "Lutz is up?" somebody cried in disbelief.

"Easy out!" yelled the girl playing first base. "No batter, no batter, no batter!" Everyone on the other team hooted and laughed. Out of the corner of my eye I saw Gail put her face in her hands.

I ground my teeth together and started praying. Please let me get a walk. Please let me get a walk. I knew I could never hit the ball. So a walk was my one and only hope.

Of course I struck out.

Four straight strikes.

"Lutz the Klutz!" I heard someone cry. Then a lot of kids laughed.

Without looking back, I marched off the baseball diamond and away from the playground. I was heading home toward the peace and quiet of my own room. It might not be perfect, I thought. But at least at home no one teased me about being a klutz.

"Hey, look, guys!" a voice shouted as I turned onto my street.

"Hey — wow — it's Lutz the Klutz!" someone else answered.

"Lookin' good, dude!"

I couldn't believe my bad luck. The three voices belonged to the biggest, meanest, toughest creeps in the entire neighborhood — Barry, Marv, and

Karl. They're my age, but at least five times as big!

These guys are *gorillas*! I mean, their knuckles drag on the sidewalk!

And when they're not swinging back and forth on a tire swing in their gorilla cage, what's their favorite activity?

You guessed it. Beating me up!

"Give me a break, guys," I pleaded. "I'm having a bad day."

They laughed.

"You want a *break*, Lutz?" one of them shouted menacingly. "Here!"

I only had time to blink as I watched a huge, mean-looking fist heading right for my nose.

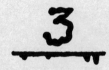

A long, painful ten minutes later, I walked through the back door of my house. Fortunately, my mom was somewhere upstairs. She didn't see my bloody nose, scratched, bruised arms, and torn shirt.

All I needed was for her to start fussing over me and threatening to call the other boys' parents. If that happened, Barry, Marv, and Karl really *would* kill me the next time they saw me.

As I crept up the stairs, Claus the cat came leaping out at me.

"Yowl!"

"Whoooooa!" I was so shocked, I almost fell back down the stairs. "Get away from me, you monster!"

I pushed the cat away and hurried down the hall to the bathroom. I gazed into the mirror and almost heaved. I looked like road kill!

I rinsed off my nose with ice-cold water. Then

I cleaned off all the blood and staggered to my room.

I took off my ripped-up T-shirt and hid it behind my bed. Then I put on a winter shirt with long sleeves. It would be hot, but it would hide my scratched arms.

Downstairs in the kitchen, I found Mom and Krissy. Mom was getting out mixing bowls and eggs, and Krissy was tying a big apron around her waist. As usual, Claus was purring and wrapping himself around Krissy's legs. Why did he act like such an innocent little kitten around her, and such a monster around me?

"Hi, Gary," my mom said to me. "You want to help us make peanut butter cookies?"

"No, thanks," I said. "But I'll lick the bowl for you later." I walked over to the table and picked up the bag of taco chips I'd left there before.

"Well, at least you can help by getting that new jar of peanut butter out of the cupboard and opening it for me," Mom said. "This recipe calls for a lot of peanut butter."

"Sounds good," I said. "Just so long as it doesn't have any honey in it."

I opened the cupboard door and took out the peanut butter. I tried to twist off the cap. I twisted as hard as I could, but the top just wouldn't move. I banged the jar on the countertop and tried again. Still no luck.

"Do you have a wrench or something around, Mom?" I asked. "This thing just won't budge."

"Maybe if you ran hot water on it," my mother began.

"Oh, puh-lease!" Krissy said with a snort. Wiping her hands on her apron, she crossed the room and grabbed the jar away from me.

With two fingers, she twisted off the cap.

Then she started laughing her head off. My mom started laughing, too.

Can you believe it? My own mother was laughing at me!

"I guess you forgot to eat your oat bran this morning," Mom said.

"I'm leaving," I muttered to Mom and Krissy. "Forever."

The two of them were laughing together. I don't think they even heard me.

Totally miserable, I stepped out the front door and slammed it hard behind me. I decided to ride my bike around the block a few times. When I went around to the side of the house and got it out of the garage, I started to cheer up a little bit.

My bike is really awesome. It's a new, blue, twenty-one speed, and it's real sleek and cool. My dad gave it to me for my twelfth birthday.

I jumped on my bike and headed down the driveway. As I turned onto the street, I saw some girls walking down the sidewalk. Out of the corner of my eye, I recognized them.

Wow! I thought. It's Judy Donner and Kaitlyn Davis!

Both Judy and Kaitlyn go to my school. They're really pretty and very popular.

To be honest, I've had a major crush on Judy since the fourth grade. And once, at the fifth-grade picnic, she actually smiled at me. At least, I think it was at me.

So when I saw those girls walking down the street, I decided it was a good time to try to be really cool.

I flipped my baseball cap around so the brim was at the back of my head. Then I folded my arms across my chest and started pedaling no-handed.

As I passed them, I glanced over my shoulder and flashed my most glamorous smile at Judy and Kaitlyn.

Before my beautiful smile faded, I felt a tug at my sneaker. I realized instantly that my shoelace was caught in the chain!

A horrible grinding sound filled the air. The bike jerked and lurched from side to side — and I lost control!

"Gary —!" I heard Judy shriek. "Gary — look out for that car!"

4

CRAAAAAAACK.

I didn't see the lamppost until I hit it.

As I toppled off my bike and shot sideways through the air, I heard the sound of metal crumpling, ripping, and shredding.

I landed on my face in a deep, warm puddle of mud.

I heard the car rumble past me.

Slowly, I pulled my face out of the mud.

Guess I didn't look too cool, I thought bitterly. Maybe at least I'll get a little sympathy.

No way.

I could hear Judy and Kaitlyn laughing behind me on the sidewalk. "Nice bike, Gary!" one of them called. They hurried away.

I had never been so humiliated in all my life. If I could have, I would have put down roots in that mud puddle and turned myself into a tree. It might

17

not be the most exciting life in the world. But at least no one laughs at a tree.

I'm serious. At that moment, I would have happily traded lives with a tree. Or a bird. Or a bug. Or just about any other living object on the planet.

With that sad thought, I decided to get myself up and out of there before anyone else came along. It took all my strength to peel my wrecked bicycle off the lamppost. Luckily, I didn't have far to drag it.

For the second time in the same afternoon, I crept into my house and up the stairs so I could get cleaned up before anyone saw me. Now, as I studied my reflection in the bathroom mirror, I saw there was no way I could hide all my cuts and scrapes from my mom.

"Oh, who cares?" I moaned as I washed the mud off my face and hands. "Who cares if Mom sees them? I'll be doing her a favor by giving her something *else* to laugh at. It'll really make her day!"

I went back into my room and changed into my last clean shirt. Then I glanced around, trying to find something to do.

I decided to boot up my computer. Playing with my computer is one of the few things I really like. When I'm lost in the world of a computer game, sometimes I can actually forget I'm a total jerk named Gary Lutz. Nobody in a computer game ever calls me Lutz the Klutz.

I turned on the computer and decided to have another try at the *Planet Monstro* Fantasy game I'd been stuck on for two days. *Monstro* is a really cool game.

When you play it, you're a character named The Warrior, and you're trapped on the planet Monstro. You have to get yourself out of all kinds of scary situations.

Before I started to play, I thought I'd check Computa Note, one of the electronic bulletin boards I'm connected to on the computer.

I'd left a message there on Monday, asking if anyone knew how to defeat the two-headed dragon that kept eating me on the thirteenth moon of Monstro. Sometimes other people in the country who are playing the same game will send each other hints.

When I accessed Computa Note, I saw the following computer-game-related messages on the screen:

To Arnold in Milwaukee: Have you tried rubbing smashed-up eucalyptus leaves all over yourself in the rain forest game? It's an ecologically correct way of repelling the poisonous ants in EcoScare 95. *From Lisa in San Francisco*

To R from Sacramento: The only way to escape from the flood on your spaceship in SpaceQuest

20 is to inflate your suit and float away. *From L in St. Louis*

To Gary in Millville: Try stabbing the dragon between the eyes. It worked for me. *From Ted in Ithaca*

Oh, terrific, I thought. I'd been *trying* to stab the dragon between the eyes. But the creature always ate me before I could do it! What was "Ted in Ithaca" doing that I wasn't?

I decided to leave another electronic note, asking Ted to explain what he meant. But, as I started typing, I noticed another message at the very bottom of the computer screen.

I read it. Then I read it again very carefully:

TAKE A VACATION FROM YOURSELF.
Change places with someone for a week!

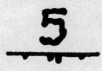

5

What could that mean?

I pressed the Enter button so I could read what was next. I desperately wanted more information about the message. This is what I saw:

TAKE A VACATION FROM YOURSELF.
Change places with someone for a week!

PERSON-TO-PERSON VACATIONS
113 Roach Street, Suite 2-B
or call 1-800-555–SWAP

How could it possibly work? I asked myself. How could two people change lives without getting into all kinds of trouble?

I had to admit it sounded totally crazy.

Crazy, but interesting.

I yawned and scratched the back of my head.

"Ouch!" My hand grazed one of the painful bumps I'd gotten from Barry, Marv, and Karl.

It really hurt. But the stab of pain helped me make up my mind. I was *definitely* ready for some changes in my life.

"I don't want to spend the rest of my life getting beat up!" I told myself. "Or crashing into lamp-posts, either! Or being the last person chosen for the team!"

I took out a piece of paper and copied the address from the screen. As I did, I realized it was only a few blocks from my school. I knew just where it was. I could stop by the Person-to-Person office the next day.

I'm really going to check it out, I decided.

Making up my mind like that improved my mood a lot. I was beginning to feel almost cheerful when I went back downstairs. But not for long. When my family sat down in the dining room for dinner, my father noticed my banged-up face.

"Gary!" he exclaimed. "What in the world happened to you?"

"Er," I said. "I had a little accident on my bike." I winced as I said the word "bike." I was thinking about the mangled wreck in the corner of the garage.

"I don't believe that for a minute," Mom said. "I'm sure you've been fighting with those big kids in the neighborhood again. Why in the world can't you children learn to settle your disagreements peacefully?"

Krissy started laughing so hard, she almost choked on her tuna casserole. "Gary doesn't have any disagreements with those guys, Mom!" she said. "They just like to beat him up!"

My mother shook her head angrily. "Well, I think that's just outrageous!" she said. "I have a good mind to call those boys' parents up right now and give them a piece of my mind!"

I groaned loudly. "I'm telling you, Mom, I really had an accident with my bike. If you don't believe me, go check it out in the garage."

Then my father *did* believe me. He started lecturing me about bike safety and why I should have been wearing my helmet and how I was going to have to pay to have the bike fixed with my own money.

After a while, I stopped paying much attention. As I pushed my casserole around on my plate, all I could think about was my plan for changing my life with Person-to-Person Vacations.

The sooner the better, I thought. The sooner I get out of this life, the better off I'll be.

We finished dinner, and I went upstairs to play on my computer again. I spent the rest of the evening with my *Planet Monstro* game.

I kept trying to stab the dragon between the eyes. But even though I followed Ted from Ithaca's advice, I couldn't do it. The dragon ate me twenty-three times.

Finally, I gave up and crawled into bed. I was so wiped out, I started drifting off to sleep almost right away. I turned over and pulled the blanket up under my chin. I curled up into a ball. The toes on my right foot touched something.

"Huh?" I said out loud. "What *is* that down there?"

My heart pounded in my chest.

Slowly, I moved my toes again.

"Ohhhhhh." My blood turned into ice.

I jumped out of bed and let out a bloodcurdling scream.

6

Frantically, I ripped the blankets off my bed. In the dim light coming in through the window, I could see the rat — fat and hairy, its red eyes gleaming at me.

I screamed again.

Then I heard laughter down the hall. Krissy's laughter.

My stomach sank. I made my way to the switch and turned on the light.

Sure enough. The rat still stared at me from my bed. But now I recognized it. A gray rubber rat. One of Claus's favorite toys.

In her room down the hall, Krissy squealed with laughter.

"I'm going to get you, you little brat!" I screamed. I thought about going down the hall and really thumping her. But I quickly decided against it.

Even though Krissy is only nine, she happens

to be pretty strong. There was an excellent chance she could beat me up.

With an angry growl, I grabbed the rat off my bed and heaved it into the corner of my room. Then, my heart still pounding with rage, I turned off the light and climbed back under the covers.

"Tomorrow," I promised myself in the dark room. "Tomorrow, you, Gary Lutz, are going to check out that ad and find out if you can change your life. Even if it's only for a week, it has to be better than this miserable life you have now!"

The next day I kept my promise to myself. After breakfast, I walked the six blocks to Roach Street and started reading the street numbers, trying to find number 113.

I guess I was looking for some kind of big, glass office building. But when I finally found number 113, it was on a small, gray building that looked something like my dentist's office. A little sign on the outside read:

PERSON-TO-PERSON VACATIONS,
Suite 2-B

I opened the door and walked up a flight of steps. At the top, I opened another door and went into a kind of waiting room with beige carpeting and tan leather chairs.

A dark-haired woman sat behind a big glass window. She smiled at me when I came in, and I walked over to talk to her.

"Good afternoon," she said into a microphone.

I jumped. Even though the woman was right in front of me, her voice came out through a speaker on the wall.

"Uh . . . um," I stammered nervously. "I came about the message on the electronic bulletin board?"

"Oh, yes," the woman replied with another smile. "A lot of people learn about us from their computers. Pardon me for staying behind this glass shield. But the equipment behind me is so delicate, we have to be very careful about protecting it."

I peered over the woman's shoulder. I could see gleaming metal counters and a wall of electronic equipment, including what appeared to be heart monitors, video screens, X-ray machines, and cameras. It looked like something right out of *Star Trek*!

I suddenly had a heavy feeling in my stomach. Maybe this is a bad idea, I thought. "Y-you probably don't like kids hanging around in here," I stammered. I started backing away toward the door.

"Not true," she said. "Many of our customers are young people such as you. A lot of kids are

27

interested in changing places with someone else for a week. What did you say your name was?"

"Gary. Gary Lutz."

"Nice to meet you, Gary. My name is Ms. Karmen. How old are you. About twelve?"

I nodded.

"Come over here for a minute," Ms. Karmen said, motioning with her hand.

Cautiously, I walked back over to the glass booth. She opened a little slot at the bottom of her window and pushed out a book. I picked it up and saw that it was a photo album, like the one my parents have from their wedding.

I opened it and started looking through it. "It's kids!" I exclaimed. "All about my age."

"Correct," said Ms. Karmen. "They're all interested in switching lives with someone else for a week."

"Wow." I studied the album.

A lot of the kids in the pictures looked big and strong. And cool. Kids like that wouldn't be afraid of anything, I told myself. I wondered what it would be like to be one of them.

"You can pick a boy — or even a girl, for that matter — to trade places with for a week," Ms. Karmen was saying.

"But how does it work?" I asked. "Do I just go take over somebody's room and live in his house for a week? Go to his school? Wear his clothes?"

The woman laughed. "It's far more interesting than that, Gary. With our getaway vacations, you actually *become* the other person for a week."

"Huh?"

"What we have," the woman explained, "is a safe, painless way to switch one person's mind into another person's body. So, while *you'll* know you're really you, no one else will recognize you. Not even the other boy's parents!"

I was still confused. "But . . . what about my body? Does it get stored here?"

"No, no. We here at Person-to-Person will find someone else to take over your body for the week. Your parents will never even know you're gone!"

I looked down at my skinny body and wondered who could possibly want to borrow it for a week. Ms. Karmen leaned forward in her chair. "So what do you say? Are you interested, Gary?"

I stared into her dark brown eyes and swallowed hard. I broke into a cold sweat. This whole thing was really weird — and *scary*! "Uh," I said. "I don't know. I mean I'm just not sure."

"Don't feel bad," Ms. Karmen said. "Many people take some time to get used to the idea of a body switch. You can think it over for as long as you wish."

She took out a small camera. "But in the meantime, would you mind if I took your picture? That way, we can find out if anyone is interested in being in your body for a week."

"Well, I guess it's okay," I replied.

She snapped the picture, and the flash went off in front of my eyes. "But I'm still not sure I want to go through with it."

"There's no obligation," Ms. Karmen said. "Why don't we leave it this way? You fill out a form describing yourself. Then I'll put your picture into our display album. And, when we find someone to take your place, I'll call you to see if you've made up your mind."

"Okay," I replied. What harm could that do? I asked myself. There was *no way* she would ever find anybody who'd want *my* body for a week!

I spent a few minutes filling out the form. I had to write down my name and address. Then I had to tell all about my hobbies, and how well I did in school, and things like that. When I was finished, I handed it to Ms. Karmen, said good-bye, and headed out the door.

I made it most of the way home without getting into trouble. A block and a half from my house, I ran into my three most unfavorite people in the world — Barry, Marv, and Karl.

"Hey, guys!" Barry cried with an ugly smile. "The Klutz is up and walking around. That must mean we didn't do a very good job of pounding him yesterday."

"No," I insisted. "You did a good job. You did a *very* good job, guys!"

I guess they didn't believe me. They all jumped me at once.

When they were finally finished — about five minutes later — I lay on the ground and watched them walk away through one swollen black eye.

"Have a nice day!" Marv called back to me. All three of them roared with laughter.

I sat up and pounded the ground with my fist.

"I'm sick of this!" I wailed. "I want to be somebody else — *anybody* else!"

Slowly and painfully, I dragged myself to my feet. "I'm doing it," I decided. "And nobody's going to stop me. Tomorrow I'm going to call Person-to-Person Vacations. I want them to put me into somebody else's body. As soon as they can!"

7

I spent the next few days changing my Band-Aids and hoping the woman from Person-to-Person Vacations would call me.

At first, I ran to answer the phone every time it rang. But of course it was never for me. Usually, it was one of Krissy's dumb friends, wanting to giggle and gossip.

One afternoon, I was reading a science-fiction book in my usual spot behind the big maple tree. I heard a sound, and peered around from behind the tree.

Sure enough, there was Mr. Andretti walking across the lawn. He was dressed in his beekeeping outfit. As I watched, Mr. Andretti went to the screened-in area off the garage and started opening up the little doors to his beehives.

Bzzzzzz.

I covered my ears, but I couldn't shut out the

loud, droning hum. How I hated that sound! It was just so frightening.

I shivered and decided it was time to go back inside.

As I climbed to my feet, a bullet-sized object shot right by my nose. A bee!

Were the bees escaping for real this time?

I gasped and stared over at Andretti's house. Then I almost choked. There *was* a big hole in the screen around the beekeeping area.

A *lot* of bees were flying out!

"Ow!" I cried out as a bee landed on the side of my head and buzzed loudly into my ear.

Frantically, I batted it away. Then I ran toward the house. For one wild moment, I thought about calling the police or maybe the paramedics.

But, as I slammed the back door, I heard an all-too-familiar sound. "Haw haw haw!"

Once again, Mr. Andretti was laughing at me.

I pounded my fist into my other hand. Oh, how I'd like to sock that guy in the nose! I thought.

I was interrupted by the sound of the phone ringing.

"Give me a break!" I cried as I stomped off to answer it. "Don't Krissy's moron friends have anything better to do than talk on the phone all day long?"

"Whaddya want?" I snarled into the mouthpiece.

"Is this Gary?" a woman's voice asked. "Gary Lutz?"

"Uh . . . yes," I answered in surprise. "I'm Gary."

"Hi, Gary. This is Ms. Karmen. From Person-to-Person Vacations? Remember me?"

My heart started thumping in my chest. "Yes. I remember," I answered.

"Well, if you're still interested, we've found a match for you!"

"A match?"

"Correct," said Ms. Karmen. "We've found a boy who wants to switch bodies with you for a week. Are you interested?"

I hesitated for a few seconds. But, then, as I gazed out the back door of the kitchen, I saw a big, fat bee throwing itself against the outside of our screen door. "Haw haw!" Mr. Andretti's scornful laughter boomed across the back yard.

My mouth tightened into a thin line. "Yes," I said firmly. "I'm really interested. When can we make the switch?"

"Why, we could do it now," said Ms. Karmen. "If that's all right with you."

My pulse raced as I thought. My parents were both out for the afternoon, and Krissy was playing at a friend's house. The timing was perfect. I'd never get another chance like this!

"Now is great!" I exclaimed.

"Terrific, Gary. It will take me about twenty minutes to get to your house."

"I'll be waiting."

The next twenty minutes seemed to take forever. While I waited, I paced back and forth in the living room, wondering what my new body would be like.

What would my new parents be like? My house? My clothes? Would I actually have some friends this time around?

By the time Ms. Karmen arrived, I was a wreck. When the doorbell rang, my hand was sweating so much, I could barely turn the doorknob to let her in.

"Let's go in the kitchen," Ms. Karmen suggested. "I like to set up my equipment on a table." She opened a small case and took out some black boxes with monitors on them.

I showed her the way to the kitchen. "So who's this kid who wants to switch places with me?" I asked.

"His name is Dirk Davis."

Dirk Davis! I thought excitedly. Even his name sounded cool. "What does he look like?"

Ms. Karmen opened up a white photo album. "Here's his picture," she said, passing it to me.

I looked down at a picture of a tall, athletic-looking blond boy in black Lycra bike shorts and a blue muscle shirt. I blinked in surprise.

"He looks like a surfer or something!" I cried. "Why in the world does he want to switch bodies with me? Is this some kind of trick?"

Ms. Karmen smiled. "Well, to be honest, it's not exactly your *body* he's interested in, Gary. He wants your *mind*. You see, Dirk needs someone who is good in math. He has some very hard math tests coming up in summer school. He wants you to take them for him."

"Oh," I said. I felt relieved. "Well, I usually do pretty well on math tests."

"We know that, Gary. Person-to-Person does its homework. You're very good at math. Dirk's good at skateboarding."

I sat down at the table.

Bzzzzzz.

A bee buzzed right under my nose. "Hey!" I yelled, jumping back up. "How'd that bee get in here?"

Ms. Karmen glanced up from her equipment. "Your back door is open just a bit. Now please sit down and try to relax. I need to fasten this strap around your wrist."

With a nervous glance at the back door, I sat back down. Ms. Karmen strapped a black band around my wrist. Then she started fiddling with some wires attached to one of her machines.

Bzzzzzz.

Another bee flew in front of me, and I wiggled around in my chair.

"Please sit still, Gary. Otherwise the equipment won't work."

"Who can sit still with all these bees buzzing around in here?" I asked. I lowered my eyes and saw three fat bees walking across the table.

Bzzzzzz.

Another bee flew past my right eye.

"What's up with these bees?" I was starting to panic.

"Don't pay any attention to them," Ms. Karmen said, "and they won't bother you." She made one more adjustment to her machine. "Besides, Dirk Davis isn't afraid of bees. And, as soon as I flip this switch, you won't be, either!"

"But . . .!"

ZZAAAAPPPP!

A blinding white light flashed in front of my eyes.

I tried to cry out.

But my breath caught in my throat.

The light grew brighter, brighter.

And then I sank into a deep pool of blackness.

8

Something was wrong.

Colors returned. But they were a total blur.

I struggled to make everything come clear. But I couldn't seem to focus on anything.

My new body didn't feel right, either. I was lying on my back, and I felt light as a feather, light enough to float away.

Could this be Dirk Davis's tall, muscular body? It certainly didn't feel like it!

Was this some kind of trick? I asked myself. Was the picture of Dirk Davis a phony? Was he really a lot smaller than he looked in the photo album?

I reached out one of my hands and tried to touch my stomach. But my hand felt really weird, too. It was small, and my arm seemed to be bending in several places at once!

What's going on? I wondered, trembling with fright.

Why do I feel so *weird*?

"Whooooa!" I cried out as I finally managed to touch my body. "Yuck." My skin was soft. And it was covered with a fine layer of fuzz.

"Help! Ms. Karmen! Help! Something's wrong!" I tried to shout.

But there was something wrong with my voice. It came out all tiny and squeaky. Little mouse squeaks.

I rolled over onto my stomach and tried to get up. I spread my arms to balance myself.

I gasped as I realized my feet weren't even touching the ground!

I was flying!

"What's happening to me?" I cried in my squeaky little voice. I floated forward and crashed into a kitchen cupboard.

"Ow! Help me!"

I moved my strange new arms and realized I had some control over which way I flew. I felt some weird muscles in my back going into action. Testing my new muscles, I flew over to the kitchen window.

Exhausted, I landed on the sill. I turned my head to one side. Then I gasped in fright.

A hideous monster was reflected in the window glass!

The creature had two huge glaring eyes. And it was staring right at me.

I tried to scream. But I was too terrified to utter a sound.

I — I have to get away! I decided.

I moved my feet and started to run. The monster in the glass ran, too.

I stopped and stared at the window glass. The monster stopped and stared back at me.

"Oh, no! Please — no!" I cried. "Please don't let it be true!" I reached up and tried to cover my eyes. The creature in the window did the same thing.

And suddenly I knew the hideous truth. The monster in the mirror — it was me.

Ms. Karmen had messed up. Totally.

And now I was trapped inside the body of a bee!

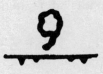

9

I don't know how long I stood there.

I couldn't stop staring at my reflection.

I kept waiting to come out of this nightmare. I kept waiting to blink my eyes and find myself in Dirk Davis's big, muscular body.

But I didn't look at all like Dirk Davis.

I had two giant eyes — one on either side of my head — and two skinny little antennas sticking out of my forehead.

My mouth was truly disgusting. I had some kind of long tongue, which I soon discovered I could move all around and make longer and shorter if I wanted. Which I didn't.

My body was covered with thick, black hair. I had three legs on either side of my body. And let's not forget the wings sticking out of my shoulders!

"This is the pits!" I cried. "I'm a bug! I'm a disgusting, hairy bug! Ms. Karmen — something went wrong! *Help me!*"

Creeeeak.

Slam!

What was that?

Oh, no! I realized that Ms. Karmen had just gone out the kitchen door.

"No — wait! Wait!" I squeaked. She was my only hope!

I had to catch her. I had to tell her what had happened!

"Ms. Karmen!" I squeaked. "Ms. Karmen!"

Frantically, I flew out of the kitchen into the living room. Out the window, I could see her car still parked out in front of the house.

But the front door to the outside was shut. And bees can't open doors. I was trapped inside my own house!

The back door! I remembered. Ms. Karmen had said it was open just a bit.

Yes! That was how all those bees got into the house in the first place!

I fluttered my new wings and flew back into the kitchen. As I soared, I realized I was getting more and more control over my flight pattern.

But I didn't care about that right now. All I knew was that I *had* to get to Ms. Karmen before she drove away.

I darted out the tiny opening in the back door. "Ms. Karmen!" I shouted as I flew around the side of the house. "Ms. Karmen! Help me! You messed up! I'm a bee! Help me!"

My voice was so tiny, she couldn't hear me. She opened her car door and started to climb behind the wheel. My only chance for a normal life was about to drive away!

What could I do? How could I get her attention?

Thinking quickly, I flew right toward her head. "Ms. Karmen!" I shouted in her ear. "It's me. Gary!"

Ms. Karmen uttered a startled cry. Then she drew back her hand and swatted me. Hard.

"Ow!" My entire body vibrated with pain. The force of her swat sent me falling to the street. I hit the pavement with a painful *splat*.

I shook my head, trying to clear my eyes. That's when I realized I had an extra set of tiny eyes arranged in a kind of triangle on the top of my head. I used them to gaze straight up.

And then I screamed in terror.

I saw the tire rolling toward me.

Ms. Karmen was about to drive right over me. I was about to be squashed like the bug that I was!

10

"Oh!" I froze in panic.

Even with my blurred bee vision, I could see the deep treads in the tire as it rolled steadily toward me.

Closer. Closer.

I have to move! I told myself.

Fly away! Fly away!

But in my panic, I forgot how to use my new muscles.

I — I'm going to be squashed! I realized.

I uttered a final, weak cry.

And the car stopped.

"Huh?" My entire body was trembling. But somehow I managed to pull myself up. Up into the air.

Yes. I was flying now.

I could see Ms. Karmen inside the car. She was fastening her seat belt. She had stopped the car to put on her seat belt!

"Hey, seat belts really *do* save lives!" I told myself.

I called out to her. But of course she couldn't hear me. I watched the car roll away until it was a blur of color.

Then, exhausted and terrified, I buzzed over to a nearby lilac bush and dropped onto a leaf. "That was too close!" I told myself, in between gasps for air. "I'm going to get killed out here!"

A green caterpillar inched its way up onto a nearby stem and started chewing noisily on the leaf I was resting on. I'd never really examined a caterpillar before. Up close, they're real ugly. They look a little bit like dragons. Only scarier.

"Keep away from me!" I yelled in my tiny voice. The caterpillar didn't even turn its head. Maybe it didn't hear me.

I forgot all about the caterpillar when I heard footsteps coming up the front walk. I turned my head and used my sideways eye to see who it was.

"Mom!" I screamed. "Mom! Over here!"

She couldn't hear me. She hurried up the steps and into the house.

Suddenly, I was overcome by a wave of sadness. My own mother didn't recognize me!

Desperately, I fluttered my wings and flew away from the leaf. I made my way to the front of the house, and started buzzing around the front windows.

I had my wings under complete control by now. But the scene I saw inside the house was enough to make me fall down onto the ground again.

My mother stood in the living room talking to *me*! Or at least, that's what she thought. Only I knew it couldn't be me. *I* was stuck outside. But who *was* in there with my mom? Had Dirk Davis managed to get inside my body?

I landed on the ledge and stared into the house. My mom was talking. The boy was nodding and laughing. He said something to her. If I stared closely, I could read his lips.

"Hey, did you buy taco chips? I'm really starving, Mom."

That had to be Dirk talking inside my body.

My mom smiled at him and patted him on the arm. I read his lips and saw that he was calling her "Mom" again. How could he do that? How could he call *my* mother "Mom"?

If bees could cry — which I now know they can't — I would have started bawling right then and there. Who did that boy think he was? For that matter, what kind of mom did I have, who couldn't even tell that a total stranger was living inside her son's body?

As I watched "myself" and my mom chatting in the living room, I totally lost it. Like a crazed maniac, I started bashing my insect body into the window.

"Buzz!" I cried. "Buzz! Buzz! Buzz! It's me, Gary. Look out here! Help me!"

Again and again, I smashed myself up against the glass. But no one inside the house noticed.

After a few minutes, Mom brought the new me a bag of taco chips. I watched "Gary" rip the bag open and take out a handful of chips. Crumbs fell on the living room carpet as he crunched the spicy chips.

I realized I was starving.

But what do bees eat? I asked myself. Desperately, I tried to remember everything I'd ever read about the creatures.

I thought of the hungry caterpillar, crunching away on the leaf. But I was almost positive bees didn't eat leaves.

But what *did* they eat? Other bugs? Ugh! The thought made me shudder. I'd *die* before I'd eat a bug!

I buzzed around the yard, hoping to see something — anything — I could use for food. As I flew, I found that I was getting used to my strange new vision and learning how to work my different sets of eyes.

I remembered something I'd once read in an old picture book called *The Big Book of Bees*. It said that bee eyes each have thousands of tiny lenses crowded together. But, because they don't have pupils, they can't really focus their eyes.

47

Interesting, I thought. But not very helpful. If I could remember about bees' eyesight, why couldn't I remember what they ate?

I settled onto another bush to think. And suddenly, I became aware of a wonderful odor nearby. I turned my head and saw a beautiful yellow flower.

Then I remembered something else I'd read. "Pollen," I said out loud. "Bees eat pollen. And they get it from flowers!"

Excitedly, I flew up into the air and started hovering over the yellow blossom. I tried to open my mouth — before I remembered I didn't have that kind of mouth anymore!

Instead, I had my long, weird tongue. But how was I supposed to use it to get the stuff out of the flower?

I didn't have a clue!

As I hummed around in the air, I realized I was becoming more and more exhausted. If I didn't get something to eat soon, I was going to faint.

I started to feel dizzy. I hardly knew where I was.

I became more and more confused. My brain got so fuzzy, I even began to wonder if I'd ever actually been a boy at all. Maybe I'd really been a bee for my entire life, and I'd just dreamed about being a boy.

Slam!

Somebody closed a car door nearby, and I was startled out of my mental fog. I swiveled my head to look.

Dad!

He was closing the garage door. Now he was walking across the driveway and heading toward the back door of the house.

"Dad!" I screamed. "Dad. It's me. Gary! Help me!"

"Hi, Gary," Dad said.

11

"Dad! You can hear me!" I cried joyfully. "Dad — you've got to help me!"

My heart sank when Dad walked right past me and started talking to the fake Gary.

Desperately, I started buzzing round and round their heads.

"Looks like Andretti's lost one of his workers," my dad laughed. He swatted at me with his rolled-up newspaper.

A near miss. I darted away.

"Uh, right," the fake Gary laughed, pretending he knew what Dad was talking about. "Andretti."

"Let's help get dinner on," my dad said. He put a friendly hand on my former shoulder. "Okay, son?"

"Sure thing, Dad."

Like best pals, my dad and his phony son crossed the lawn and opened the screen door.

"Wait!" I shouted. "Wait!"

Like a space rocket, I shot through the air after them. If I really put the speed on, I thought I could make it through the door before it closed. Fast, faster, and . . .

BLAM!

The screen door banged shut, right on top of my tiny bee body. Once again, I sank into a deep pool of blackness.

"Ohhhhhh. Where am I? What happened? Am I still a bee?"

Dazed, I fought my way back to the real world. When I was able to get my eyes open, I realized I *was* still a bee — a small, frail, slightly damaged bee — who'd just narrowly missed being scrunched by a screen door.

Now I was lying on my back on the grass in our yard. My six legs were thrashing the air.

"I was a klutz as a human — and I'm a klutz as a bee!" I wailed. I tried to flip myself over. "I've only been a bee for an hour, and I've almost been killed. Twice!"

I suddenly knew what I had to do. I had to get to Ms. Karmen's office and tell her what had happened.

I didn't know if I could do it. But I knew I had to try.

I let out a small grunt, and with a huge effort, flipped over onto my stomach. Using all five of my eyes, I checked myself out. Both sets of wings seemed to be working. And all my six legs were still there.

"Okay," I told myself. "You can do it. Just fly to the Person-to-Person office and go inside."

I flapped my wings and started to take off into the air. But I'd only risen about an inch up off the ground when I heard a sound that made my blood run cold.

It was Claus the cat. With his long, sharp claws extended, he leaped through the air.

I let out a squeal as he pounced on me, grabbed me in one paw, and began to tighten his claws around my body.

12

As the cat's claws closed around me, I saw his hideous mouth gape open.

Sting him! Sting him!

The thought burned into my mind.

But something held me back. Something told me not to use my stinger.

I suddenly remembered something else I'd read in *The Big Book of Bees*. Honeybees die once they use their stingers!

No way! I thought.

I was still hoping to come out of this alive. And back in my old body.

So, if using my stinger was out, I'd have to use my wits instead.

With a loud gnashing of his teeth, Claus snapped his huge mouth shut. He lowered his head, preparing to snap up his furry prize — me.

At just the right moment, I burst out of his

claws and ducked out from under his gnashing teeth.

I tried to shoot off through the air. But the cat whipped out his paw and batted me down.

Claus was playing with me as if I were one of the chewed-up catnip mouse toys Krissy always gives him for Christmas.

With my last burst of strength, I spread my wings, shot up through the air, and flew as fast as I could. A backwards look out of one of my eyes told me that I'd left the surprised cat sitting in the grass.

For one second, I experienced a wonderful sensation of triumph. "You did it, Gary!" I crowed to myself. "You, a tiny little bee, managed to fight off a great big vicious cat!"

I was so pleased with myself, I decided to take a little victory lap. I spread my wings out wide and began a big, slow circle in the air.

Whap!

Oh, no! Now what?

I'd crashed right into something! But what was it? It wasn't hard, like a wall or a tree. Instead, it was soft and clinging, like cloth. And my feet were all tangled up in it.

I struggled to squirm free. I wiggled and pushed. But my legs were caught.

I was trapped.

"Haw haw haw!"

The booming laughter made my entire body shake.

I suddenly realized where I was.

I was caught in Andretti's net.

A wave of despair made me slump against the white netting.

I knew exactly what would happen next.

He would put me in his hives — and I would never get away.

13

"Time to go back home now, my little buzzing babies," Mr. Andretti sang. "Time to get back to work, my honeys." He started to laugh at his stupid pun. "My honeys! Haw haw! Oh, my, wasn't that a good one?"

Bzzzzz. Bzzzzzzz.

From the loud humming sounds in my ears, I knew I wasn't the only bee Andretti had caught in his net. In fact, out of my right eye, I could see another bee who looked just like me. He loomed right in front of me, and wiggled his antennas in my face.

Whooa! What a monster!

My wiry legs began trembling with fright. I twisted myself around and around, struggling to get away from him.

I finally got myself turned the other way. But then I saw I was facing another bee. And another. Each one looked scarier than the last.

They all had big, bulging eyes and creepy antennas! And they all buzzed menacingly at me.

The frightening hum grew louder and louder as Mr. Andretti caught more bees in the net. Suddenly, the net began to shake. Up and down, up and down — like a violent earthquake — until I couldn't even think straight!

As the net shook, I lost my footing and fell into a big, squirming cluster of bees at the bottom of the net.

Whooooa! I stumbled over the pile of wriggling, hairy bees. And as I staggered in terror, bees fell on top of me.

A crawling, buzzing nightmare!

I've never been so terrified. I screamed in my tiny voice. I tried to climb up the side of the net, but my feet were stuck under another bee's body. How I hated the feel of his disgusting fuzz!

In my terror, I knew I had to escape. I had to get away from here. I had to get to Ms. Karmen's office and beg her to help me.

Then I had the most terrifying thought of all. If I couldn't escape, I suddenly realized, I would remain a bee for the rest of my life!

As Mr. Andretti carried me and the other bees across his back yard, I started buzzing and shivering with panic. How could this have happened to me? I asked myself. How could I ever have been so stupid as to try to change bodies with somebody else? Why wasn't I happy with the perfectly good body I'd already had?

Mr. Andretti opened the door to the screened-in area off the side of his garage. "We're back now, my little honeys," he cooed.

The net started to shake, and I figured out that Mr. Andretti was slowly turning it inside out. One by one, he started plucking us — his prisoners — off the side of the mesh cloth and plopping each one back inside his hanging drawer hives.

As Andretti reached for the bees, they started buzzing louder than ever. Finally, it was my turn to be plucked out of the net.

When I saw the ends of Andretti's grasping fingers reaching for me, I hung back, clinging to the net. I suddenly remembered his bragging speech about how he never used gloves because his bees "trusted" him.

I watched his fingers stretch toward me.

It would be so *cool* to plunge my stinger into his soft, plump skin, I thought.

Should I do it?

Should I sting him?

Should I?

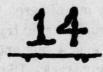

14

I didn't sting him.

I really didn't want to die.

Sure, things really looked terrible for me right now. But I was still clinging to a shred of hope.

Maybe, somehow, I'd find my way out of this bee prison and back into my own body. It didn't seem very likely. But I was determined to keep on trying.

"In you go, my fuzzy little friend," Mr. Andretti said. He opened up one of the removable drawerlike parts of his hive and dropped me in.

"Ohhhh," I moaned. It was so dark inside the hive. And so confusing.

Where should I go? What should I do?

The air was hot and wet. Everywhere I turned, I was surrounded by a deafening, droning hum.

"I — I can't *stand* it!" I cried. I could feel myself totally losing it!

All around me, bees scurried around in the darkness. I stayed where I was, too frightened to move.

I suddenly realized I was still very hungry. If I didn't get something to eat, I knew I'd never be able to find a way out of here!

I spun around and started trying to explore.

Out of my left eye, I saw another bee glaring at me. I froze in my tracks. Did bees attack each other inside their hives? I wondered.

I didn't remember reading anything about that in my bee book. But this bee really looked ready for a fight.

"Please leave me alone," I begged in my tiny voice. "Please give me a break."

The bee glared back at me. I've never seen such big, angry-looking eyes!

Slowly, I started backing away from him. "Uh . . ." I squeaked nervously. "I've got to be going now. I . . . um . . . I have to get to work."

The bee bulged his eyes and waved his antennas in a threatening way. I was sure he planned to sting me. I turned and flew away as fast as I could. I tried to hide.

I was so frightened, I couldn't even make myself move. What if I bumped into another bee? I couldn't even stand to think about what might happen if I did.

I realized I had to move. I had to find something to eat.

Shaking with fear, I tiptoed out into the open. I took a nervous look around.

On the far wall, I could see a large cluster of bees, busily building something. A honeycomb!

And where there was a honeycomb, I told myself, there was honey.

I've always hated the sweet, sticky goo. But I knew I had to eat some. Right away!

As quietly as I could, I crept over and joined the bee workers. Out of the corner of my eye, I saw them doing really gross things with their mouths.

First, they used their legs to pick little flakes of waxy-looking stuff off their abdomens. Then they crammed the wax into their mouths and started working their jaws up and down like little chewing machines. Finally, they spit out the wax and used it to build part of the honeycomb they were working on.

"Yuck!" It looked so disgusting. It made me sick!

But what choice did I have? I had to eat some honey — even if it was covered with bee spit.

I turned my head and practiced sucking my tongue up and down. Then I slurped up a big puddle of honey.

Amazing! For the first time in my life, I actually liked that stuff. Soon, I was sucking it down as if it were chocolate milk.

After a while, I got quite good with my tongue, which was actually more of a bendable tube than a tongue. It was really the perfect tool for guzzling honey.

If I ever made it back to the outside world, I thought I'd now be pretty good at using it for gathering nectar and pollen. Why, I might turn out to be the best worker in the whole hive!

I tried to smile, and then I almost gagged on my honey.

What was happening to me?

What was I thinking? I was actually starting to feel like a bee!

I *had* to get out of this place. Before it was too late!

I wanted to start searching for an escape route right away. But I suddenly felt so tired. So completely worn out . . .

Was it the honey? Or was it the strain of so much fear?

I could barely keep my eyes open. The droning hum grew louder.

With a weary sigh, I sank against a clump of hairy bodies.

I sank into the warm darkness of the hive, surrounded by the steady buzz. Breathing the sweet aroma of the honey, I sank beside my furry brothers and sisters.

I'm one of them now, I told myself weakly. I'm not a boy anymore. I'm a bee. A buzzzzzzzzzing bee. A bee sinking into the warm, dark hive. My home.

Sinking . . . sinking . . .

15

I woke up with a start and tried to brush a bee away from my face. It took me a few moments to remember. I wasn't lying in my back yard anymore, trying to keep the bees away from me. I was a bee — a bee trapped inside a hive!

I jumped up, took a step, and immediately came face to face with another bee! I couldn't tell if he was the same one I'd seen the night before. But he looked just as angry. His big eyes were bulging with rage. And he was moving deliberately toward me.

As fast as I could, I spun around and flew away. Of course, I had no idea where I was going.

The hive seemed to be made up of a lot of long, dark hallways. All around me, groups of bees were building honeycombs. As they worked, they kept up a steady buzz. The sound was really driving me off the wall!

I began searching for a way out. I wandered in

and out, in and out throughout the dark, sticky honeycombs.

From time to time, I shot out my tongue and lapped up some honey. I was getting a little tired of the sweet stuff. But I knew I had to keep up my strength if I wanted to try to break out of the hive.

As I searched for a way to escape, I noticed that every single bee seemed to have an assigned job, either building honeycombs, caring for the babies of the queen or whatever. And the little bugs never stopped working! They were "busy as bees" from morning till night.

Darting through the tangled darkness, I began to lose hope.

There's no way out, I decided. No way out.

I sank unhappily to the sticky hive floor. And as I dropped, three large bees moved in front of me.

They buzzed angrily, bumping up against me with their hairy, damp bodies. It was easy to tell these bees were angry with me.

Maybe it was because I wasn't doing my "job." But what *was* my job? How could I tell the bees I didn't know what I was supposed to be doing?

I tried to slip past them, but they moved to block my path.

Three tough bees. They made me think of Barry, Marv, and Karl.

I shrank back as one of them pointed his stinger at me.

He was getting ready to kill me! And I didn't even know what I'd done!

I screamed and whirled around. As fast as my six legs would carry me, I darted back down the narrow passageway and turned another corner.

"Oh!" I bumped hard into another bee. Luckily, he was hurrying off somewhere, and barely seemed to notice me.

I gasped with relief. And then an idea came to me. Where was that bee going in such a hurry? Was he taking something somewhere? Could he be going to an area I hadn't searched yet?

I decided to follow him and find out. I needed to learn everything I could about the hive. Maybe, just maybe, it would help me escape.

I hurried after the bee. I thought I'd find him quickly. But he was already long gone.

I searched in and out among the different honeycombs, but I couldn't find him anywhere. After a while, I gave up.

Way to go, Lutz the Klutz, I scolded myself. I felt worse than ever.

I shot out my tongue and slurped up a big helping of honey to keep myself going. Then I began my endless searching again.

"Whoooa!" I stopped when I reached an area that looked familiar. I was pretty sure it was the place where Andretti had dropped me when he first put me into the hive.

All at once, a large group of angrily buzzing bees crowded against me.

"Hey —!" I protested as they shoved me forward.

They replied with a sharp, rising buzz.

What were they doing? Were they attacking me? Were they all going to sting me at once?

They had me surrounded. I couldn't run away.

But how could I possibly fight off all these bees? I was doomed, I realized. Finished. Sighing in defeat, I closed my eyes and started to shake.

And waited for them to swarm over me.

16

I waited to be crushed.

And waited some more.

When I opened my eyes, the angry bees had moved to the side of the hive. They weren't paying any attention to me.

I saw a single bee, standing in the center of the hive floor. He was performing a kind of jumping, twisting, hip-hop dance.

How weird! I thought. The other bees were watching intently, as if this were the most interesting thing in the world.

"Those bees didn't care about me," I told myself. "They were trying to get me out of the way so this bee could do his dance."

I realized I'd wasted a lot of time. I had to keep searching for an escape route.

I tried to push myself away from the group of bees, but the hive floor had become too crowded to move.

The bee danced faster and faster. He moved his body toward the right. All the other bees stared intently at him.

What was going on?

At that moment, something from my old *Big Book of Bees* came back to me. I remembered that bees send out scouts to find their food. Then the scouts "dance" to tell the other bees where to go get it!

If the scout was reporting on where to get food, it meant he'd just been out of the hive. That meant there had to be a way out of this place!

I was so excited, *I* almost started dancing!

But I didn't have a chance because, suddenly, all the bees in the hive rose up like a dark cloud. I spread my wings and flew up with them.

As I followed, the bees formed a single, orderly line and shot out through a tiny hole in a far, upper corner of the hive.

I buzzed around until I found the end of the line. Then I got ready to escape.

Would I make it?

The very last bee in line, I shot out of the tiny hole into open space. For a few seconds, I watched the other bees floating away, busily hunting for nectar and pollen.

I knew I looked just like them. The difference was that they would willingly return to Andretti's hive. But I never, ever would. At least, not if I could help it.

"I'm out!" I cried joyfully in my tiny voice. "I'm out! I'm free!"

Dazzled by the sudden bright light of the outer world, I flew around and around in the beekeeping area. Then I headed for the hole I'd seen in the screen when I was still in my own body.

I knew it was on the wall that faced my family's yard. But when I flew over to it, I stopped and gasped in disappointment.

The hole had been patched up. Mr. Andretti had fixed it!

"Oh, no!" I wailed. "I can't be trapped! I *can't* be!"

My heart started thumping crazily. My whole body was vibrating.

I forced myself to calm down and look around.

None of the other bees were in the screened-in area anymore. They'd already gone outside to collect pollen. And that meant there had to be another way out.

I wasn't thinking clearly because I was exhausted, worn out from all my flying around. I sat down on top of the hive to rest.

At that instant, the door between the beekeeping area and the garage opened. "Good morning, my little bee friend," Mr. Andretti's voice boomed. "What are you doing, lying around on top of the hive? Why aren't you busy inside making me some honey? Are you sick? You know we can't have any sick bees around here."

As I gazed up weakly, Mr. Andretti moved closer. His huge, dark shadow fell over me.

I tried to curl up into a ball and disappear. But it was no use. His large fingers were stretching right toward me!

I yelled in terror. But of course, he couldn't hear me. What is he going to do to me? I asked myself. What does he *do* with sick bees?

17

What does he do with sick bees? I wondered again, quivering in terror.

He probably throws them in the garbage, I thought. Or even worse — he feeds them to his pet bird or frog.

Despite my weariness, I knew I couldn't wait around to find out. I had to get out of there!

Just as Mr. Andretti's fingers were about to fold around me, I shot up into the air and buzzed around his head. At the same instant, I saw some other bees flying in through a tiny hole in the screen. It was in the corner, near the ceiling.

I buzzed Mr. Andretti's face one more time. Then I raced toward the hole. As I tried to squeeze myself out the exit hole, I crashed right into another bee who was flying in. He glared at me and gave me an angry buzz.

Frightened, I backed off and clung to the screen. I had to wait for a long line of bees to come back inside. It seemed to take them forever.

When I was finally sure the last bee had come in, I leaped forward and shot out of the hole. I was out in the open sky!

"This time I really *am* free!" I screamed in celebration, forgetting my weariness. "And Andretti's never going to catch this bee again!"

I landed on a leaf and let the morning sun warm my back and wings. It was a beautiful day — a beautiful day for finding somebody who could help me get back into my human body!

Like a rocket, I shot straight up into the air and gazed around. I recognized the familiar creak of my father opening the back door of my house.

Panting hard, I raced forward.

My father called, "Good-bye, hon! Tell the kids I'll see them tonight!" over his shoulder and let go of the door.

I darted into the house. The door slammed hard. Another near miss.

I hummed with happiness. It felt so good to be back in my own house and out of that dark, sticky hive! I landed on the counter and gazed around at the old, familiar walls.

Why hadn't I ever realized how nice my house was before?

Step, step, step.

Someone was coming into the kitchen! I flew up onto the windowsill for a better look.

Krissy!

Maybe I could get her to listen to me.

"Krissy! Krissy!" I buzzed. "Over here by the window. It's me, Gary!"

To my delight, she turned and stared in my direction.

"Yes!" I cried excitedly. "Yes — it's me! It's me!"

"Oh, terrific," Krissy groaned. "One of Andretti's dumb bees got in here again."

Okay, so it wasn't exactly the reaction I'd been hoping for. But she'd still noticed me! Maybe, I thought, if I flew right onto her shoulder and spoke into her ear, she'd be able to understand me!

My heart vibrating my entire body, I lifted myself up off the windowsill and soared toward my sister. "Krissy!" I buzzed as I approached her shoulder. "You have to listen to me!"

"Aaaaiii!"

Krissy screeched so loud, I was afraid the glass in the windows would shatter. "Get away from me, bee!"

She started thrashing her hands in the air, trying to bat me away.

"Ow!" I cried out as she slapped me. Stung with pain, I lost control and landed with a thud on the tiled countertop.

I raised my eyes in time to see Krissy grab a flyswatter from out of the broom closet.

"No, Krissy, no!" I screamed. "Not that! You don't want to do that to your own brother!"

My sister lifted up the flyswatter and thwacked it down right next to me. I could feel the rush of air from it. And I felt the entire counter shake.

I screamed and quickly rolled to one side.

Krissy, I knew, was a menace with a flyswatter.

She was the champion in our family. She never missed.

The eyes on top of my head spun in terror. And in the gray blur, I could see the shape of the flyswatter, rising up to slap me again. And again.

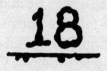

18

"Stop, Krissy!" I screamed. "Stop! You're squashing me!"

With a strangled gasp, I toppled off the counter. I hit the floor hard and struggled dizzily to my feet.

Now I started to get angry. Why did Krissy have to be so bloodthirsty? Couldn't she just open a window and shoo me out?

Buzzing weakly, I floated up off the floor. Regaining my strength, I began darting wildly around the room, crashing into the walls and cupboards to show Krissy how upset I was. Then I shot out of the kitchen.

In a rage, I headed up the stairs to my room. If my sister wouldn't help me, I'd get someone else to help. Namely, the new Gary!

The morning sun was high in the sky. But "Gary" was still sound asleep in *my* bed.

Seeing him lying there so peacefully, so completely at home, made me even angrier.

"Wake up, you slug!" I buzzed at him. He didn't move. His mouth hung open as he slept, making him look like a real jerk.

"Yuck! What a creep!" I was sure my mouth never hung open when *I* slept!

I decided to take action. I landed on "Gary's" head and started walking around on his face. I was sure my little insect legs would tickle him and wake him up.

Nothing. He didn't move.

Even when I stuck a leg up his nose, "Gary" slept without stirring.

"Why is he so wrecked?" I wondered. "Has he been wearing out my body?"

Furious, I ran across "Gary's" face and climbed down through his hair. Then I crawled onto his ear. "BUZZ!" I shouted as loudly as I could. "BUZZ! BUZZ! BUZZ!"

Incredible as it seems, the new "Gary" didn't even budge.

Just my luck. Dirk Davis was turning out to be the world's soundest sleeper!

I sighed and gave up. I crawled off "Gary's" ear and flew around my old room, gazing down at my bed, my dresser, and my computer.

"My computer!" I cried excitedly. "Maybe I can

put a message on the screen! Maybe I can tell my parents what has happened to me!"

I swooped down to the computer, buzzing eagerly.

Yes! The computer had been left on.

What luck! I knew I wasn't heavy enough to push the Power button.

Would I be strong enough to type?

A clear blue screen greeted me on the monitor. My heart pounding, I lowered myself to the keyboard and started hopping around on the letters.

Yes! I was heavy enough to make the keys go up and down.

I paused, resting on the Enter key.

What should I type? What message should I put on the screen?

What? What? What?

As I frantically thought, I heard "Gary" stir behind me on the bed. He let out a groan. He was waking up.

Quick! I told myself. Type something! Type *anything*!

He'll see it as soon as he gets out of bed.

I hopped over to the letters and began to jump up and down, spelling out my desperate message.

It was hard work. My bee eyes weren't made for reading letters. And I kept leaping up and falling in the cracks between the keys.

After eight or nine jumps, I was gasping for air.

But I finished my message just as "Gary" sat up in bed and stretched.

Floating up in front of the monitor, I struggled to read what I had typed:

I AM NOT BEE. I AM GARY. HELO ME.

Through my blurred vision, I saw that I missed the P in HELP and hit the O instead. I wanted to go back and fix it. But I was totally wiped out. I could barely buzz.

Would they understand?

Would they read the message and see me standing on top of the monitor and understand?

"Gary" would understand. I knew he would. Dirk Davis would figure it out.

I climbed wearily to the top of the monitor and watched him climb out of bed.

Here he comes, I saw eagerly. He brushed his hair out of his eyes. He yawned. He stretched again.

Over here! I urged.

Dirk — please — check out the computer monitor!

Dirk — over here!

He picked up a crumpled pair of jeans off the floor and pulled them on. Then he found a wrinkled T-shirt to go with it.

Come on, Dirk! I pleaded, hopping up and down on top of the monitor. *Read the screen — please?*

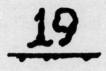

19

Would he read it?

Yes! Rubbing his eyes, "Gary" shuffled over to the computer.

Yes! Yes!

I nearly burst for joy as I watched him squint at the screen. "Go ahead, Gary! Read it! Read it!" I squeaked.

He squinted at the screen some more, frowning. "Did I leave that thing on overnight?" he muttered, shaking his head. "Wow. I must be losing it."

He reached down and clicked off the power. Then he turned and made his way out of the room.

Stunned, I toppled off the monitor, landing hard on the desk beside the keyboard. All that work for nothing.

What was "Gary's" problem, anyway? Doesn't he know how to read?

I've got to talk to him, I told myself, pulling

myself together. I've got to communicate with him somehow.

I lifted my wings and floated up after him. I followed him through the kitchen, and then slipped through the back door with him.

As he strode across the grass, I started buzzing around his head. But he didn't pay any attention to me.

He crossed the yard and opened our garage door. Then he went inside and brought out my old skateboard.

I hadn't used that skateboard in at least two years. My uncle had given it to me for my tenth birthday, and I almost broke my leg trying to ride it. After that, I put it away and refused to touch it again.

"Don't get on that thing!" I yelled at "Gary." "It's dangerous. You might hurt my body. And I want it back in one piece!"

Of course "Gary" didn't even notice me. Instead, he carried the skateboard out in front of the house and put it down on the ground.

A short while later, Kaitlyn and Judy walked up the sidewalk. I waited for them to start giggling and making fun of the new me.

"Hi, Gary," Kaitlyn said. She brushed some curly hair off her forehead and smiled. "Are we late for our skateboarding lesson?"

"Gary" flashed her a big smile. "No way, Kaitlyn," he answered in my voice. "Want to head over to the playground like we did yesterday?"

I couldn't believe my ears. Skateboarding lesson? Head over to the playground *like we did yesterday*? What was going on around here?

"I hope you don't mind, Gary," Judy said. "We told some of the other kids — like Gail and Louie — how good you are. They all said they can't wait to take a lesson from you, too. Is that okay? Because if it isn't, we can call them, and —"

"No problem, Jude," "Gary" broke in. "Let's get going, okay?" The new "me" hopped onto his skateboard and smoothly rolled his way down the sidewalk. Judy and Kaitlyn hurried after him.

For a second, I was too shocked to move. But then I decided to follow them.

As I swooped after them, I kept muttering to myself, "I can't believe it! Lutz the Klutz is giving skateboard lessons at the playground? Everybody's waiting for him to show up? What is going on?"

A few minutes later, the four of us had reached the playground. Sure enough, a whole gang of kids was waiting there for "Gary." He put down his skateboard and started giving everybody pointers on "boarding," as he called it.

I buzzed over to him and started shouting in his ear again. "Dirk!" I shouted. "Dirk Davis! It's me. The real Gary Lutz!"

Very casually, he swatted me away.

I tried to speak to him again. This time he swatted me really hard, sending me spinning to the ground.

Trying to shake off the pain, I gave up. Dirk isn't going to help me, I realized.

Ms. Karmen is my only hope. After all, she was the one with all the equipment. She was the only person who could reverse what she had done.

I flew onto a tree and tried to figure out which way to fly. When you're an insect, everything looks different to you. Things that seem small to a person appear huge to a bee. So I wanted to be sure I didn't get myself mixed up and fly off in the wrong direction.

Standing on a big leaf, I gazed up and down the block until I was sure I knew which way to go. As I got ready to take off, a large shadow suddenly loomed over my head. At first, I thought it was a small bird. But then I realized it was a dragonfly.

"Stay calm," I told myself. "A dragonfly is an insect, isn't it? And insects don't eat each other, right?"

I guess no one had told the dragonfly.

Before I could move, it zoomed down, wrapped its teeth around my middle, and bit me in two.

20

I uttered a last gasp and waited for everything to go dark.

It took me a few seconds to realize that the dragonfly had turned and buzzed off in the other direction.

My imagination was running away with me. That's what always happened when I got over-tired.

I took a deep breath, grateful to still be in one piece. I decided I had to use my remaining strength to get to Ms. Karmen at the Person-to-Person Vacations office.

I rose up into the air, looked both ways for oncoming dragonfly traffic, then fluttered away.

After a long, tiring trip, I floated past a street sign that told me I'd made it to the right block. Roach Street.

I buzzed along the sidewalk until I came to the Person-to-Person building. Then I sat down on the stoop and tried to figure out how I was going to get inside.

Luckily, as I rested on the warm cement, I saw a mailman marching up the street, stopping at each house along his route. Quickly, I flew over to the Person-to-Person entrance and checked it out. Just as I'd hoped, there was a mail slot in the middle of the door.

I buzzed over to the doorknob, and waited for my chance. Slowly, the mailman trudged up to the building.

"Hurry up!" I screamed at him. "Do you think I have all day here?" Of course he couldn't hear me.

He fumbled around in his bag and pulled out a bundle of letters. Then, slowly, he reached out and pushed open the mail slot.

Before the mailman had a chance to react, I swooped down in front of his nose and buzzed right through the mail slot. As I zipped along, I heard him gasp, and I knew he'd seen me. But for once, luck was with me. I moved so quickly, there hadn't been any time for the mailman to try to swat me.

My luck held when I flew up the stairs.

I'd just reached the top when the door to Person-to-Person Vacations opened, and a girl about my age came out. She had long, curly red hair and had a serious, thoughtful expression on her face. Was she thinking of trading places with someone?

"Go home!" I shouted at her. "And don't come back. Stay away from this place! Just look what happened to me!"

Even though I was screaming, the girl didn't even turn her head. But she left the door open just long enough for me to buzz into the Person-to-Person office.

I flew across the waiting room and saw Ms. Karmen, sitting in the same chair she'd been in when I first met her.

I shot right toward her — and smacked into something hard.

Pain roared through my body. I dropped to the floor, dizzy and confused.

As my head began to clear, I remembered the glass wall separating Ms. Karmen from the waiting area. Like some kind of brainless June bug, I'd crashed right into it!

I shook myself to clear my mind. "Ms. Karmen!" I yelled. "Ms. Karmen. It's me — Gary Lutz. Look what happened! Can you help me? *Can* you?"

21

Ms. Karmen didn't even glance up from her paperwork. Once again, I realized no one could hear my squeaky insect voice.

With a defeated moan, I sank down onto the seat of the chair and curled up into a tiny ball. I'd come all this way for nothing, I realized. I'd found the one person in the world who might be able to help me. And she couldn't even hear me!

"I give up," I whispered sadly. "It's hopeless. I have to get used to the idea of being a bee forever! There's no way I'll ever get my old body back."

I had never been so miserable in all my life. I wished someone would come along, drop into the chair, and sit on me!

A strange sound startled me from my unhappy thoughts. I sat up straight and listened hard.

"Whoo-ah. Whoo-ah." It almost sounded like someone breathing. But how could that be? It was so loud!

I floated up off the chair and buzzed around the room, trying to find out where the sound was coming from. I had circled the room twice before I figured it out.

Ms. Karmen was bending over to pick up something she'd dropped on the floor. Her nose and mouth were only inches from the top of her desk. And the microphone she used to talk to people had picked up the sounds of her breathing!

Suddenly, I had a brilliant idea. If I could get to the other side of the glass, I could use the microphone to make Ms. Karmen hear me.

I swooped over to the wall and flew straight up to the ceiling. No luck there. The sheet of glass went all the way up. There was no space for me to wedge myself through to the other side.

I buzzed down to the place where the glass met the top of Ms. Karmen's desk. Yes! There was a small slot in the glass. I remembered how she had passed through the book of photographs on my first visit to the office.

The slot wasn't very large. But it was plenty big enough for my round little bee body.

I shot through the hole and jumped up on top of the microphone.

"Ms. Karmen!" I shouted, putting my mouth next to the hard metal. "Ms. Karmen!"

Her eyes opened wide. Her mouth dropped open in confusion. She stared out into the waiting room, searching for the person speaking.

"It's Gary Lutz!" I called out. "And I'm down here on your microphone."

Ms. Karmen stared down at the microphone. Then her eyes narrowed in fear. "What's going on? Who's doing this? Is this a joke?"

"No!" I cried. "It's no joke at all. It's really me — Gary Lutz!"

"But — but —" she stammered, but no other words came out. "What's the joke? How are you doing that?"

Her voice was so loud, the sound waves nearly blasted me off the microphone.

"You don't have to yell!" I cried. "I can hear you."

"I don't *believe* this!" she exclaimed in a trembling voice. She stared down at me.

"It's all your fault!" I shouted angrily. "You messed up the transfer operation. When you made the switch, one of my neighbor's bees must have gotten into the machine. So, instead of putting me into Dirk Davis's body, you put me into a bee!"

Ms. Karmen blinked. Then she slapped her forehead. "Well that explains it!" she cried. "That explains why Dirk Davis's body has been behaving so strangely."

She picked up some papers on her desk and started putting them into her briefcase. "I really must apologize," she said. "I feel really bad, Gary. We've never had a mix-up like this before. I hope . . . I hope it's at least been *interesting* for you."

"Interesting?" I shrieked. "It's been a nightmare! You wouldn't believe what I've been through. I've been attacked by screen doors, cats, flyswatters — you name it! You yourself almost ran me over with your car!"

All the color drained from her face. "Oh, no," she cried, her voice a whisper. "I'm so sorry. I — I didn't know."

"Well, what about it?" I asked her impatiently.

"What about *what*?"

"What about getting me back into my body! Can you do it right away?"

Ms. Karmen cleared her throat. "Well, I *could*," she replied slowly. "Normally, I could transfer you right back. But there's a slight problem in your case."

"What kind of problem?" I demanded.

"It's Dirk Davis," Ms. Karmen replied. "It seems he's become very attached to your old body. He likes your house and your parents, too. In fact, he even likes your sister, Krissy!"

"So?" I cried. "So what's that supposed to mean?"

Ms. Karmen stood up and pushed in her desk chair. "It *means*," she said, "that Dirk Davis is refusing to give up your old body. He says he absolutely won't go back to his old life. He plans to keep your body forever."

22

"*WHAT?*" I screamed, hopping up and down angrily on the microphone.

"Just what I said," Ms. Karmen said. "Dirk Davis wants to keep your body for the rest of his life."

"But he can't do that, can he?"

"It is very upsetting," she replied, biting her lower lip. "It wasn't what he said in our original agreement. But if he refuses to get out of your body and your life, there's really nothing I can do."

Ms. Karmen gazed down at me sympathetically. "I'm so sorry about this, Gary," she said softly. "I guess I'll have to be more careful in the future."

"What about *my* future? What am I supposed to do now?" I wailed.

Ms. Karmen shrugged. "I don't know. Maybe you could go back, wait in the hive — and maybe Dirk Davis will change his mind."

"Back to the hive?!" My antennas stood straight on end, quivering with rage. "Do you have any idea what it's like in there? Cramped together with those hairy bees in the darkness? Listening to that deafening buzz day and night?"

"It's a way of staying alive," Ms. Karmen replied bluntly.

"I — I don't care!" I stammered. "I'm never going back there! Never!"

"This is tragic. Tragic!" Ms. Karmen cried. "I'll give your case some thought tonight, Gary. I promise. Maybe I can come up with a way of getting your body away from Dirk."

She crossed the room and opened the office door. "I'm so upset. So upset," she murmured. Then she disappeared out the door, slamming it behind her.

Trembling with anger at Dirk Davis, I hopped down to the desk. "Hey, wait!" I called after her. "You've locked me in!"

Ms. Karmen was so upset, she forgot about me!

I rose up into the air and started after her. But, then, I happened to glance back down at her desk. Dirk Davis's questionnaire was right on top of a pile of papers. His address was next to his name. He lived at 203 Eastwood Avenue.

Eastwood Avenue was near the computer store, so I knew where it was. "Maybe the *old* Dirk

Davis will know how to get my body back!" I told myself.

It was worth a try. I ducked through the slot in the glass and flew around the waiting room.

No exit. No open window. No crack in the door.

Once again, I was trapped.

Frantically, I buzzed all around the waiting room. Then I went back through the slot in the glass. I checked out the whole equipment room. Every window was closed tight.

I flew past a calendar and happened to see the date. "Oh, no!" I cried. "It's Friday! It's the weekend. Ms. Karmen might not come back to work for two whole days."

In two days, I realized, I would starve to death!

I *had* to get out! I went over to the far wall and noticed another door I hadn't seen before. I zipped through it.

The room turned out to be a tiny bathroom. With one small window. Which was open just a crack. It was all I needed.

"Hurray!" I yelled. I shot out through the window and sailed into the open air. Then I turned right and headed for Eastwood Avenue. Luckily, it wasn't very far away. All this flying around was really beginning to wear me out.

I found Dirk Davis's house without any trouble. When I got there, I saw "Dirk" himself — or whoever he was now — standing in the front yard. I recognized him from the picture I'd seen in the Person-to-Person album.

"Hey!" I yelled to him. "Hey, er . . . Dirk!"

The tall, good-looking boy turned around and stared at me. His mouth moved, and it looked as if he was saying something.

But I couldn't understand any words. All I heard was a humming sound.

"I'm Gary Lutz!" I cried in my little voice. "Can you help me get Dirk Davis out of my body?"

The boy stared at me. Then he grinned.

I was confused. What was he grinning about?

"Hey, you can hear me!" I cried.

Now "Dirk" motioned with his hand.

"You want me to follow you?" I asked. I felt excited. "Are you taking me someplace where we can get help?"

"Dirk" grinned again. Then he turned and walked around the corner of the house. I didn't know where we were going. But I knew I had to follow him.

I found "Dirk" in the back yard. "Hum," he said to me. "Hum." He pointed to a big rosebush and grinned. Then he stuck his nose deep inside one of the blossoms. "Hummmmmmmmm," he said. "Yummmmmm."

I gaped at him in shock. "Of course!" I cried.

"You got the bee's mind when I got the bee's body!"

"Dirk" didn't say anything. But when he pulled his face out of the rose, the end of his nose was covered with yellow pollen.

"Dirk" looked a little surprised. And disappointed. I guess he missed his long, sucking tongue — the tongue that was now hanging off the front of *my* face.

"You can't help me," I muttered to him. "You're in worse shape than I am!"

"Hum?" he replied. "Hum?"

He looked kind of silly with that yellow nose. But I felt sorry for him. He and I had the wrong brains in the wrong bodies. I knew exactly how he felt.

"I'm going to go get help for both of us," I told him. "If I get my body back, maybe you'll get yours, too."

With a loud buzz, I flew out of the Davises' yard. As I left, I thought I heard "Dirk" buzz back at me. I glanced over my wing and saw him sticking his face into another rose. Maybe this time he'd have better luck getting the pollen out.

I headed toward my own house. This time I planned to *make* Dirk Davis give me my body back. Or else.

As I turned up my street, I suddenly heard a familiar voice coming from behind a tree.

"Don't mess with me! Don't mess with me, man!"

I couldn't believe it. The voice belonged to Marv. But who was he talking to?

I shot around the tree to find out. To my surprise, I saw that Marv was talking to *me* — or, Dirk Davis, in my body. Barry and Karl were right beside him.

Look out, Dirk! I thought. Run! Run!

Please don't let them wreck my body!

But I was too late.

Barry, Marv, and Karl were closing in on him, about to give him the pounding of his life.

23

I flew closer.

"Look out, Dirk! Look out!" I squeaked.

But to my surprise, the three hulking creeps weren't moving in on "Gary" — they were *backing away* from him!

"Don't mess with me!" Marv cried. "I *said* I was sorry."

"We apologized," Barry whined. "Don't hit us again, Gary! Please!"

Karl whimpered behind him, nursing a bloody nose.

"You guys are losers," I heard "Gary" tell them. "Take a hike. Go get a life."

"Okay! Okay!" Marv cried. "Just no more rough stuff, okay, Gary?"

"Gary" shook his head and walked away.

I don't *believe* this! I thought gleefully. Barry, Marv, and Karl were afraid of *me*!

I decided I'd have some fun with them, too.

I swooped down and landed on Barry's nose, buzzing as loudly and menacingly as I could.

"Yowwwww!" he shrieked in surprise — and swatted himself on the nose.

I was too fast for him. I was already on Karl's ear.

Karl cried out and toppled backwards into a thorny rosebush.

Then I buzzed round and around Marv.

"Get away!" he shouted angrily.

And I flew right into his mouth.

His scream nearly deafened me. But it was worth it.

Marv started spitting and choking and gagging.

I flew up into the air, laughing so hard, I nearly popped my antennas. That was the most fun I'd had since becoming a bee!

I watched the three gorillas run away. Then I flew up the block to my house.

"Gary" had left the window open, and I was able to shoot in. He was lying on my bed, reading one of my comic books and eating crackers with honey on them.

The honey smelled really good, and I realized I was hungry again. I reminded myself to stop by a flower and get a snack the next time I went outside.

But, meanwhile, I had work to do. I flew over and landed on Gary's earlobe.

"Hey, you! Dirk Davis!" I yelled at the top of my little voice. "I need to talk to you!"

He reached a hand up and flicked me off his face. I fell down and landed with a bounce on the bed.

I buzzed angrily and shot right back up to his earlobe. "Hey, you! I want my body back! You have to get out of it. Now!"

"Gary" folded up his comic book and swung it at me. I buzzed with rage and frustration. I wasn't going to give up this time. No way! I had to make him hear me.

I rocketed up in the air and landed on the top of his head. Then I climbed down to his other earlobe and tried one more time. "I'm not leaving you alone till you get out of my body!" I screeched. "Do you hear me?"

He sighed and shrugged his shoulders. "Will you *please* quit bothering me?" he asked. "Can't you see I'm trying to relax?"

"You can *hear* me?"

"Yeah. Sure," he muttered. "I can hear you okay."

"You can?" I was so surprised, I almost fell off his ear.

"Yes, I can hear you perfectly. Weird, huh? I'm not sure why. But I think some bee cells got mixed up with my human cells during our electronic transfer. I can hear all kinds of little bug noises now."

"*Your* human cells? Those are *my* human cells!" I cried.

Dirk shrugged.

"Enough chitchat," I told him. "When do you plan to get out of my body?"

"Never," he replied. He picked up his comic book and started reading it again. "I like your body. I can't understand why you gave it up to go become a bee."

"That wasn't my idea!" I screamed.

"You've got a good life here," he continued. "I mean, you have great parents. Krissy is an okay sister. And Claus is an awesome cat. Too bad you didn't know all that when you were in your body. Which is now *my* body!"

"It's not your body! It's mine! Give it back!" I started to buzz furiously all around his head, swooping down in front of his nose, crashing into his ears, batting my wings in his eyes.

Dirk Davis didn't even flinch.

"What's the matter with you, anyway?" I yelled. "You're *me* now. You're supposed to be scared of bees!"

"Gary" laughed. "You've forgotten something," he said. "I'm *not* you. I'm just inside your body. I'm still me inside. And I'm not the least bit afraid of bees!"

"And, now," he went on, "take a hike, okay? Buzz off. I'm busy."

Frozen with anger and disappointment, I slumped on the bedspread without moving. "Gary" raised the comic book up into the air. "I'd hate to swat you," he said. "But I will if I have to!"

I dodged away just as the comic book slapped down on the bedspread. Then I shot back out the window.

For a few minutes, I flew aimlessly around, lost in my sad thoughts. Finally, I remembered how hungry I was. I perched on top of a big, orange lily blossom and started sucking up some nectar.

Not bad, I told myself as I drank. But honey on crackers would be much better.

"What am I supposed to do now?" I asked myself. "Am I really doomed to be a bee for the rest of my life?" I pulled my head out of the orange blossom and looked around. "And how long *is* the rest of my life anyway?"

I remembered a page from *The Big Book of Bees*.

"The life of the average bee is not very long. While the queen can live through as many as five winters, the workers and drones die off in the fall."

In the fall?

It was already nearly August!

If I stayed in this bee body, I had only a month or two at most!

I gazed sadly up at my house. "Gary" had turned the light on in my room, and it twinkled in the early evening dusk.

How I wished I could be up there! Why, why had I ever been stupid enough to think I'd be better off in someone else's body?

Then I heard a buzz. I peered over the blossom. Sure enough, I saw a bee.

He hopped up onto the flower. Two other bees quickly joined him. Then three more. They buzzed angrily.

"Go away!" I cried.

I tried to fly away.

But before I could lift off, they all swarmed over me.

I couldn't move. The bees had taken me prisoner.

"Don't take me back to the hive!" I shrieked. "Don't take me back!"

But to my horror, they started to drag me away.

24

I struggled to squirm away. But they turned their stingers on me.

Were they some kind of bee police? Did they think I was trying to escape the hive?

I didn't have a chance to discuss it with them. They lifted me up into the air. There were bees in front of me, bees behind, and bees on all sides.

We flew past my bedroom window. "Help!" I called.

"Gary" glanced up from his plate of crackers and honey. He smiled and waved at me.

I was so angry, I thought I might explode.

But then an idea came to me. A crazy idea. A desperate idea.

I buzzed as loudly as I could. Then I darted out of line and shot into the open bedroom window.

Were the others following me? Were they?

Yes!

They didn't want to let me escape.

"Gary" sat up when he saw me and my buzzing followers. He rolled up his comic book, preparing to swat us.

I circled the room, and the other bees followed.

"Get out! Get out!" "Gary" screamed.

There weren't enough of us, I decided. I needed a huge swarm.

I flew back out the window. The others buzzed after me.

Now I was the head bee. As fast as I could, I led my group back to Mr. Andretti's garage, and in through the hole in the screen.

I hesitated at the hive entrance. I took a deep breath.

Was I really going to go back inside?

I knew I had no choice. "Go for it, Lutz!" I shouted to myself.

I shot in through the entrance hole.

Then I began flying crazily through the hive, buzzing angrily, bumping the walls, bumping other bees.

The hive stirred to life.

The buzzing grew to a dull roar. Then a loud roar. Then a *deafening* roar!

Round and round I raged, flying faster, faster, throwing myself frantically against the sticky hive walls, tumbling, darting, buzzing furiously.

The entire hive was in an uproar now.

I had turned the bees into an angry swarm.

Out of the hive I flew. Out into the darkening evening. Out through the hole in the screen, up, up, and away.

And the bees swarmed after me, like a black cloud against the gray-blue sky.

Up we soared. Up, up.

A buzzing, swarming funnel cloud.

Up, up.

I led them up to the bedroom window.

Tumbling over each other, raging through the air, we swarmed into "Gary's" room.

"Huh?" He jumped off the bed.

He didn't have time to say a word.

I landed in his hair. The raging swarm followed, buzzing angrily, surrounding him, covering his head, his face, his shoulders.

"H-help!" His weak cry was drowned out by the roar of the bees. "Help me!"

I dropped down onto the tip of Gary's nose. "Have you had enough?" I demanded. "Are you ready to give me back my body?"

"Never!" he cried. "I don't care what you do to me! You'll never get your body back! It's mine, and I'm keeping it forever!"

Whoooa! I could not believe my ears.

I mean, he was *covered* in bees! And still he wouldn't listen to reason!

I didn't know *what* to do.

The other bees were starting to lose interest.

Some of them drifted to the plate of honey. Most of them floated back out the open window.

"You can't get away with this, Dirk!" I screamed.

With a furious wail, I whirled around. Then I stabbed my razor-sharp stinger deep into the side of "Gary's" nose.

"Owwwwwww!" He let out a high-pitched shriek and grabbed at his nose.

Then he staggered backwards and fell over onto the bed.

"Yaaaaay!" I cried out in celebration.

For one instant, I felt triumphant.

A tiny bee had defeated a huge enemy! I was victorious! I had won a fight against a giant!

My celebration didn't last very long.

I suddenly realized what I had done. And I remembered what happens to a honeybee after it stings someone.

"I'm going to die," I murmured weakly. "I stung someone, and now I'm going to die!"

25

Weaker.

I felt the strength drain from me.

Weaker and weaker.

"What have I done?" I asked myself. "I gave up my life for the chance to sting Dirk Davis! Why was I such a jerk?"

I struggled to keep my wings moving, struggled to stay in the air.

I knew I was doomed. But I wanted to stay alive as long as I could. Maybe, I thought, as I felt my strength fading, maybe I'll have a chance to tell my family good-bye.

"Mom! Dad! Krissy!" I buzzed faintly. "Where are you?"

It was hard to breathe. I felt so tired, so weak.

I floated out the window and sank to the grass below.

I thought I recognized the shape of the old maple tree where I used to read books and spy on Mr. Andretti. But my sight was so bad, it was hard to be sure about anything. The whole world swirled in gray shadow.

I could no longer hold up my head. The gray shadows grew darker and darker.

Until the world faded completely from view.

I sat up slowly. The ground spun beneath me.

Where was I?

My back yard?

I blinked, struggling to bring it all into focus, waiting for my eyes to clear.

"There's the old maple tree!" I cried. "And there's my house! And there's Mr. Andretti's house!"

Was I alive?

Was I really alive, sitting in my back yard, seeing all the familiar places?

Did I have my strength back?

I decided to test it. I tried to spread my wings and fly up into the air.

But for some reason, my wings didn't seem to be working. My body felt heavy and strange.

I frowned and looked down, inspecting myself to see what was wrong. "Whoooa!" I cried out in surprise. Instead of six legs, I saw two arms and two legs and my skinny old body.

Breathlessly, I reached up to touch my face. My extra eyes were gone — and so were my antennas, and my layer of feathery fuzz. Instead, I felt hair! And smooth, human skin!

I jumped up and shouted for joy. "I'm a person again! I'm me! I'm me!"

I threw my arms around my chest and gave myself a hug. Then I danced around the back yard, testing my arms and legs.

They worked! They all worked!

I couldn't get over how wonderful it was to be human again!

"But how did it happen?" I asked myself. "What happened to Dirk Davis?"

For a chilling instant, I wondered if Dirk had been forced into a bee's body the way I had.

Probably not, I decided.

But what had happened?

How did I get my body back?

Was it the bee sting? Did the shock of the sting send us all back to the bodies we belonged in?

"I've got to call Ms. Karmen and find out!" I realized.

But for now, all I wanted to do was see my family.

I hurried up the back steps and into the house. As I ran through the kitchen, I crashed right into Krissy. As usual, she was carrying Claus under one arm.

"Watch where you're going!" Krissy snapped at me.

She probably expected me to snap back at her and try to push her out of my way. But instead I grabbed her shoulders and gave her a big hug. Then I planted a kiss on her cheek.

"Yuck! Gross!" she cried and wiped the cheek with her hand.

I laughed happily.

"Don't give me your cooties, creep!" Krissy cried.

"You're a creep!" I replied.

"No, *you're* a creep!" she repeated.

"You're a jerk!" I shouted.

It felt so good to be calling her names again!

I gleefully called her a few more things. Then I hurried upstairs to see my parents.

I met them as they were coming out of my room.

"Mom! Dad!" I cried. I hurried to them, planning to throw my arms around them.

But they thought I was just trying to get into my room. "Don't go in there, Gary," warned my dad. "You left your window open again, and a swarm of bees got in there."

"You'd better go next door," Mom said. "Get Mr. Andretti. He'll know how to get them out."

I couldn't hold back any longer. I threw my arms around my mother's neck and gave her a big kiss. "Mom, I missed you so much!"

My mother hugged me back, but I saw her exchange a curious look with my dad. "Gary?" she asked. "Are you okay? How could you miss me when you've been right here in this house?"

"Well . . ." I thought fast. "I meant that I missed spending time with you. We really need to do more things together."

My mother spread one hand over my forehead. "No. No temperature," she told my father.

"Gary," Dad said impatiently. "Would you mind running over and getting Mr. Andretti? If we don't get those bees out of your room, you'll never be able to go to sleep tonight!"

"Bees?" I said casually. "Hey, no problem. I'll take care of them."

I reached out and started to open my door. Before I could, Dad grabbed my arm. "Gary!" he cried in alarm. "What's the matter with you? There are bees in your room! B-E-E-S. Don't you remember — you're scared of bees!"

I stared back at him and thought about what he'd said. To my surprise, I realized I was no longer the slightest bit scared of bees! In fact, I was actually looking forward to seeing them again.

"No problem, Dad," I told him. "I guess I must have outgrown that, or something."

I opened the door and went into my room. Sure enough, there was the old swarm, buzzing away over the plate of honey and crackers on the bed.

"Hi, guys!" I said cheerfully. "Time to leave now!"

I walked over to the bed and waved my hands at them, trying to shoo them back out the window. A few of them buzzed angrily at me.

I laughed to myself. Then I picked up the plate of crackers and honey and dumped it out the window. "Go get it!" I told them.

I shooed them gently out the window.

"Good-bye!" I called to them as they left. "Thanks! Take good care of the honeycombs! I'll try to come visit as soon as I can!"

When the last bee was gone, I turned around and saw my parents. They were standing absolutely motionless in the doorway, staring at me, frozen with shock.

"Dad?" I said. "Mom?"

My dad blinked and seemed to come back to life. He crossed the room and put a hand on my shoulder. "Gary? Are you feeling all right?"

"Just fine," I replied, grinning happily. "Just fine."

26

That whole crazy adventure happened about a month ago.

Now it's nearly fall. I'm sitting in my favorite place under the maple tree in the back yard, reading a book and chomping down taco chips.

I just love coming out here. All the fall flowering plants are in bloom, and the yard is really pretty.

I've been spending the last few days of my summer vacation relaxing back here. Of course, I also go to the playground a lot.

The other day I ran into that girl with the red hair I saw coming out of the Person-to-Person office. We started talking, and I didn't trip over my own feet or anything. She seems very nice. I hope she doesn't plan to switch lives with anybody else!

That conversation and a lot of things have made me realize that my short life as a bee really changed me.

First of all, it taught me to appreciate my family for the first time ever. My parents are pretty nice. And my sister is okay. For a sister.

And now, I'm not scared of any of the things I used to be scared of. Yesterday, I walked right by Marv, Barry, and Karl, and I didn't bat an eye.

In fact, when I remembered how I buzzed them, I almost burst out laughing.

I'm not at all scared of them anymore. And I'm different in other ways, too.

I'm a lot better at sports and bike riding and things. And I'm a great skateboarder now. In fact, I still give lessons. Judy and Kaitlyn hang around me all the time. And Gail and Louie, too.

The other day, I actually ran into Dirk Davis at the playground. At first, I didn't want to talk to him. But then he turned out to be pretty nice.

He apologized to me. "I'm sorry I tried to steal your body," he said. "But things didn't turn out so well for me, either. That bee flunked all my math tests in summer school!"

We both had a good laugh about that. And now Dirk and I are friends.

So all in all, my life is back to normal.

I feel terrific, totally normal.

In fact, I feel much better than normal.

It's so great to sit here in the back yard, reading and relaxing, smelling the fresh fall air, enjoying the flowers.

Mmmmmm.

Those hollyhocks are really awesome.

Excuse me a moment while I get up and take a closer look.

That blossom down near the ground is so perfect.

I think I'll get down on my knees to take a quick taste.

Do you know how to suck the pollen out?

I've figured out the best way. It's not as hard as it looks.

You just pucker your lips and stick your tongue way out like this, see?

Then you dip your face down into the blossom and suck up all the pollen you want.

Try it.

Go ahead.

Mmmmmmmm.

Go ahead. It's easy. Really!

ADD MORE

Goosebumps®

TO YOUR COLLECTION...

HERE'S A CHILLING PREVIEW OF THE
NEW COLLECTOR'S EDITION OF

MONSTER BLOOD

1

"I don't want to stay here. Please don't leave me here."

Evan Ross tugged his mother's hand, trying to pull her away from the front stoop of the small gray-shingled house. Mrs. Ross turned to him, an impatient frown on her face.

"Evan — you're twelve years old. Don't act like an infant," she said, freeing her hand from his grasp.

"I *hate* when you say that!" Evan exclaimed angrily, crossing his arms in front of his chest.

Softening her expression, she reached out and ran her hand tenderly through Evan's curly carrot-colored hair. "And I *hate* when you do that!" he cried, backing away from her, nearly stumbling over a broken flagstone in the walk. "Don't touch my hair. I hate it!"

"Okay, so you hate me," his mother said with a shrug. She climbed up the two steps and knocked on the front door. "You still have to stay here till I get back."

"Why can't I come with you?" Evan demanded, keeping his arms crossed. "Just give me one good reason."

"Your sneaker is untied," his mother replied.

"So?" Evan replied unhappily. "I like 'em untied."

"You'll trip," she warned.

"Mom," Evan said, rolling his eyes in exasperation, "have you ever seen *anyone* trip over his sneakers because they were untied?"

"Well, no," his mother admitted, a smile slowly forming on her pretty face.

"You just want to change the subject," Evan said, not smiling back. "You're going to leave me here for weeks with a horrible old woman and —"

"Evan — that's *enough*!" Mrs. Ross snapped, tossing back her straight blond hair. "Kathryn is not a horrible old woman. She's your father's aunt. Your great-aunt. And she's —"

"She's a total stranger," Evan cried. He knew he was losing control, but he didn't care. How could his mother do this to him? How could she leave him with some old lady he hadn't seen since he was two? What was he supposed to do here all by himself until his mother got back?

"Evan, we've discussed this a thousand times," his mother said impatiently, pounding on his aunt's front door again. "This is a family emergency. I really expect you to cooperate a little better."

Her next words were drowned out by Trigger, Evan's cocker spaniel, who stuck his tan head out of the back window of the rented car and began barking and howling.

"Now *he's* giving me a hard time, too!" Mrs. Ross exclaimed.

"Can I let him out?" Evan asked eagerly.

"I guess you'd better," his mother replied. "Trigger's so old, we don't want him to have a heart attack in there. I just hope he doesn't terrify Kathryn."

"I'm coming, Trigger!" Evan called.

He jogged to the gravel driveway and pulled open the car door. With an excited yip, Trigger leaped out and began running in wide circles around Kathryn's small rectangular front yard.

"He doesn't *look* like he's twelve," Evan said, watching the dog run and smiling for the first time that day.

"See. You'll have Trigger for company," Mrs. Ross said, turning back to the front door. "I'll be back from Atlanta in no time. A couple of weeks at the most. I'm sure your dad and I can find a house in that time. And then we'll be back before you even notice we're gone."

"Yeah. Sure," Evan said sarcastically.

The sun dipped behind a large cloud. A shadow

fell over the small front yard.

Trigger wore himself out quickly and came panting up the walk, his tongue hanging nearly to the ground. Evan bent down and petted the dog's back.

He looked up at the gray house as his mother knocked on the front door again. It looked dark and uninviting. There were curtains drawn over the upstairs windows. One of the shutters had come loose and was resting at an odd angle.

"Mom — why are you knocking?" he asked, shoving his hands into his jeans pockets. "You said Aunt Kathryn was totally deaf."

"Oh." His mother's face reddened. "You got me so upset, Evan, with all your complaining, I completely forgot. Of *course* she can't hear us."

How am I going to spend two weeks with a strange old lady who can't even hear me? Evan wondered glumly.

He remembered eavesdropping on his parents two weeks earlier when they had made the plan. They were seated across from each other at the kitchen table. They thought Evan was out in the backyard. But he was in the hallway, his back pressed against the wall, listening.

His father, he learned, was reluctant to leave Evan with Kathryn. "She's a very stubborn old woman," Mr. Ross had said. "Look at her. Deaf for twenty years, and she's refused to learn sign language or to lip-read. How's she going to take care of Evan?"

"She took good care of you when *you* were a boy," Mrs. Ross had argued.

"That was thirty years ago," Mr. Ross protested.

"Well, we have no choice," Evan heard his mother say. "There's no one else to leave him with. Everyone else is away on vacation. You know, August is just the worst month for you to be transferred to Atlanta."

"Well, excuuuse me!" Mr. Ross said, sarcastically. "Okay, okay. Discussion closed. You're absolutely right, dear. We have no choice. Kathryn it is. You'll drive Evan there and then fly down to Atlanta."

"It'll be a good experience for him," Evan heard his mother say. "He needs to learn how to get along under difficult circumstances. You know, moving to Atlanta, leaving all his friends behind — that isn't going to be easy on Evan either."

"Okay. I said okay," Mr. Ross said impatiently. "It's settled. Evan will be fine. Kathryn is a bit weird, but she's perfectly harmless."

Evan heard the kitchen chairs scraping across the linoleum, indicating that his parents were getting up, their discussion ended.

His fate was sealed. Silently, he had made his way out the front door and around to the backyard to think about what he had just overheard.

He leaned against the trunk of the big maple tree, which hid him from the house. It was his favorite place to think.

Why didn't his parents ever include him *in their discussions?* he wondered. If they were going to discuss leaving him with some old aunt he'd never seen before, shouldn't he at least have a say? He learned all the big family news by eavesdropping from the hallway. It just wasn't right.

Evan pulled a small twig off the ground and tapped it against the broad tree trunk.

Aunt Kathryn was weird. That's what his dad had said. She was so weird, his father didn't want to leave Evan with her.

But they had no choice. No choice.

Maybe they'll change their minds and take me to Atlanta with them, Evan thought. *Maybe they'll realize they can't* do *this to me.*

But now, two weeks later, he was standing in front of Aunt Kathryn's gray house, feeling very nervous, staring at the brown suitcase filled with his belongings, which stood beside his mother on the stoop.

There's nothing to be scared of, he assured himself.

It's only for two weeks. Maybe less.

But then the words popped out before he'd even had a chance to think about them: "Mom — what if Aunt Kathryn is mean?"

"Huh?" The question caught his mother by surprise. "Mean? Why would she be mean, Evan?"

And as she said this, facing Evan with her back to the house, the front door was pulled open, and Aunt Kathryn, a large woman with startling black hair, filled the doorway.

Staring past his mother, Evan saw the knife in Kathryn's hand. And he saw that the blade of the knife was dripping with blood.

Trigger raised his head and began to bark, hopping backward on his hind legs with each bark.

Startled, Evan's mother spun around, nearly stumbling off the small stoop.

Evan gaped in silent horror at the knife.

A smile formed on Kathryn's face, and she pushed open the screen door with her free hand.

She wasn't anything like Evan had pictured. He had pictured a small, frail-looking, white-haired old lady. But Kathryn was a large woman, very robust, broad-shouldered, and tall.

She wore a peach-colored housedress and had straight black hair, pulled back and tied behind her head in a long ponytail that flowed down the back of the dress. She wore no makeup, and her pale face seemed to disappear under the striking black hair, except for her eyes, which were large and round and steely blue.

"I was slicing beef," she said in a surprisingly deep voice, waving the blood-stained kitchen knife. She stared at Evan. "You like beef?"

"Uh . . . yeah," he managed to reply, his chest still fluttery from the shock of seeing her appear with the raised knife.

Kathryn held open the screen door, but neither Evan nor his mother made any move to go inside. "He's big," Kathryn said to Mrs. Ross. "A big boy. Not like his father. I used to call his father Chicken. Because he was no bigger than a chicken." She laughed as if she had cracked a funny joke.

Mrs. Ross, picking up Evan's suitcase, glanced uncomfortably back at him. "Yeah . . . he's big," she said.

Actually, Evan was one of the shortest kids in his class. And no matter how much he ate, he remained "as skinny as a spaghetti noodle," as his dad liked to say.

"You don't have to answer me," Kathryn said, stepping aside so that Mrs. Ross could get inside the house with the suitcase. "I can't hear you." Her voice was deep, as deep as a man's, and she spoke clearly, without the indistinct pronunciation that some deaf people have.

Evan followed his mother into the front hallway, Trigger yapping at his heels. "Can't you get that dog quiet?" his mother snapped.

"It doesn't matter. She can't hear it," Evan replied, gesturing toward his aunt, who was heading to the kitchen to put down the knife.

Kathryn returned a few seconds later, her blue eyes locked on Evan, her lips pursed, as if she were studying him. "So, you like beef?" she repeated.

He nodded.

"Good," she said, her expression still serious. "I always fixed beef for your father. But he only wanted pie."

"What kind of pie?" Evan asked, and then blushed when he remembered Kathryn couldn't hear him.

"So he's a good boy? Not a troublemaker?" Kathryn asked Evan's mother.

Mrs. Ross nodded, looking at Evan. "Where shall we put his suitcase?" she asked.

"I can tell by looking he's a good boy," Kathryn said. She reached out and grabbed Evan's face, her big hand holding him under the chin, her eyes examining him closely. "Good-looking boy," she said, giving his chin a hard squeeze. "He likes the girls?"

Still holding his chin, she lowered her face to his. "You've got a girlfriend?" she asked, her pale face right above his, so close he could smell her breath, which was sour.

Evan took a step back, an embarrassed grin crossing his face. "No. Not really."

"Yes?" Kathryn cried, bellowing in his ear. "Yes? I *knew* it!" She laughed heartily, turning her gaze to Evan's mother.

"The suitcase?" Mrs. Ross asked, picking up the bag.

"He likes the girls, huh?" Kathryn repeated, still chuckling. "I could tell. Just like his father. His father always liked the girls."

Evan turned desperately to his mother. "Mom, I can't stay here," he said, whispering even though he knew Kathryn couldn't hear. "Please — don't make me."

"Hush," his mother replied, also whispering. "She'll leave you alone. I promise. She's just trying to be friendly."

"He likes the girls," Kathryn repeated, leering at him with her cold blue eyes, again lowering her face close to Evan's.

"Mom — her breath smells like Trigger's!" Evan exclaimed miserably.

"Evan!" Mrs. Ross shouted angrily. "Stop it! I expect you to cooperate."

"I'm going to bake you a pie," Kathryn said, tugging at her black ponytail with one of her huge hands. "Would you like to roll out the dough? I'll bet you would. What did your father tell you about me, Evan?" She winked at Mrs. Ross. "Did he tell you I was a scary old witch?"

"No," Evan protested, looking at his mother.

"Well, I am!" Kathryn declared, and once again burst into her deep-throated laugh.

Trigger took this moment to begin barking ferociously and jumping on Evan's great-aunt. She glared down at the dog, her eyes narrowing, her expression becoming stern. "Look out or we'll put *you* in the pie, doggie!" she exclaimed.

Trigger barked even harder, darting boldly toward the tall, hovering woman, then quickly retreating, his stub of a tail whipping back and forth in a frenzy.

"We'll put him in the pie, won't we, Evan?" Kathryn repeated, putting a big hand on Evan's shoulder and squeezing it till Evan flinched in pain.

"Mom —" he pleaded when his aunt finally let go and, smiling, made her way to the kitchen. "Mom — please."

"It's just her sense of humor, Evan," Mrs. Ross said uncertainly. "She means well. Really. She's going to bake you a pie."

"But I don't want pie!" Evan wailed. "I don't like it here, Mom! She hurt me. She squeezed my shoulder so hard —"

"Evan, I'm sure she didn't mean to. She's just trying to joke with you. She wants you to like her. Give her a chance — okay?"

Evan started to protest but thought better of it.

"I'm counting on you," his mother continued, turning her eyes to the kitchen. They could both see Kathryn at the counter, her broad back to them, hacking away at something with the big kitchen knife.

BLOOD, BLOOD, EVERYWHERE...

While staying with his weird great-aunt Kathryn, Evan visits a funky old toy store and buys a dusty can of monster blood. It's fun to play with at first, and Evan's dog, Trigger, likes it so much, he eats some!

But then Evan notices something weird about the green slimy stuff—it seems to be growing.

And growing.

And growing.

And all that growing has given the monster blood a monstrous appetite...

About the Author

R.L. Stine's books are read all over the world. So far, his books have sold more than 300 million copies, making him one of the most popular children's authors in history. Besides Goosebumps, R.L. Stine has written the teen series Fear Street, the funny series Rotten School, as well as the Mostly Ghostly series, The Nightmare Room series, and the two-book thriller *Dangerous Girls*. R.L. Stine lives in New York with his wife, Jane, and Minnie, his King Charles spaniel. You can learn more about him at www.RLStine.com.

The Original Bone-Chilling Series

Now with All-New Behind-the-Screams Author Interviews and More!